What's Italian Fo

D. A. Blake

ISBN: 9798386305567

www.publishnation.co.uk

Chapter One

WEDNESDAY

Father Joseph Boletti didn't want to die. After spending many of his fifty-nine years assuring his flock of all the glories to come, of all the rewards waiting for them, he knew that just now he wanted to cling on to his mortal existence with every ounce of his being.

His glasses had fallen off, but, even without them, he could see the blade protruding from his somewhat rounded stomach. Father Joseph's black shirt concealed the blood that seeped from the wound. Yet already it was pooling on the cold, wooden floor on which he lay.

He considered crying out for help, but the thick, sturdy door to the sacristy had been quietly and carefully closed. Besides, he didn't really have the energy now. He glanced around him, looking for a solution. The room was a blur. Losing his glasses and all this blood really wasn't helping him right now, he realised. A row of altar boy robes hung tantalisingly near him. If he could just grab one, he wondered, maybe it could help stem the blood?

As his arm flailed about unsuccessfully, it happened against something sharp. He winced as he lifted his broken glasses towards him, hardly able to believe his luck. Surely this would help him escape from this undeserved predicament, he resolved, optimism suddenly surging through him.

Determined more than ever to postpone eternal salvation for just a little bit longer, Father Joseph stared hopefully through his cracked lenses. The room came obediently into focus, revealing the familiar trappings and paperwork of his life – the large, framed painting of the Sacred Heart, various crucifixes, the chalices, the altar linens. On the table next to him, but now out of his line of vision, were the hymn books, the Mass sheets, the rotas for parishioners to sign up to, a couple of photographs from a recent parish pilgrimage to Walsingham.

Father Joseph had been very late to the party when it came to technology, and much of it still remained a mystery to him. However, he did own a mobile phone, and he knew that it currently lay on the table in that very room, balanced precariously on top of a pile of hymn books. And for that he was grateful. Better there than lost beneath a pile of crumpled Mass sheets. Or lying smashed and broken on the ground beside him. He had wanted to preserve the phone and its contents at all costs. He had needed it to be found if the worst should happen.

Despite the horror of that moment; despite the confusion and terror, the blur of movement around him, the figure in retreat; despite the searing agony radiating up through his body, when his only inclination had been to clasp at the source of the pain; despite his legs starting to give way beneath him, buckling under the weight of unimaginable shock and distress; despite all of this, Father Joseph had managed to release his grip on the phone in his hand, allowing it to fall onto the table he was still standing next to, unable to move his feet since being caught unawares in such a brutal manner. He had barely caught a glimpse of the phone, perched on high where it had landed, when the room had turned on its head all around him, and the floor had risen mercilessly to meet him.

Yet now his efforts had rendered his only means of contact with the outside world unobtainable.

How to get to that phone, he wondered? Could he somehow tip the table over?

Yet even as Father Joseph reached out again, his light-headedness began to overwhelm him and, as his senses slowly faded, his gaze fell upon a large eye, roughly spray-painted onto the wall opposite him.

Father Joseph Boletti would be found some time later with a perplexed expression on his cold, waxy face.

Chapter Two

Robert Sloane did not like churches. The dank, gloomy silence, the vague mustiness competing with lingering incense, the endless reminders of a barbaric death, the sense of guilt that would always permeate him to the core. They all combined to create an overwhelming sense of unease in him. He entered the church reluctantly via the wide, arched entrance at the very back of this place of worship, the precise point where many a journey towards an enduring union, or an eternal oblivion, had begun.

He knew exactly where the Confessional Box was, tucked away in a quiet alcove towards the back of the church. He saw it immediately. Did anybody even go to Confession these days, he wondered? My goodness, mine would be a lengthy session, he mused gloomily. His footsteps echoed almost defiantly, disturbing the peace of the deserted building, as he began his approach towards the opulent altar. He was an intruder here; a wary, grudging visitor.

The church's magnificent organ lay silent, a beast that had never in all honesty been allowed to reach its full potential, with good intentions invariably triumphing over ability. Robert was no musician, but he, like the others, had been all too aware of this back then. They had always hoped that their stance – heads down, shoulders quietly shaking – would perhaps be mistaken for religious fervour, or at the very least, would provide some sort of amusement for the bored amongst the congregation. It wasn't like they could change their outfits every week, and the script was pretty much set in stone. He remembered how they would always try to wear the most outlandish footwear they had, small acts of defiance and individuality, a shock of colour or a row of studs daringly emerging from beneath the folds of the heavy white robes.

Now, moving slowly, with what could best be described as an inherent sense of foreboding, and reverence despite himself, Robert cast his eyes across towards the statue of the Virgin Mary, resplendent in blue, arms outstretched, a welcome oasis amongst the dreary depictions of pain and suffering. How many times had he knelt before this benevolent figure, imploring, bargaining, even raging at times? Back then, her warmth had seemed to shine down upon him. He had placed his trust in her; he had counted on her. Now, as he grew tentatively closer, his gaze, detached yet vulnerable, seemed only to be met with unseeing eyes.

Lost in his reverie, Robert barely noticed the heavy, wooden door near the altar slowly opening. A figure emerged, inconspicuous in the gloom; concealed in the shadows.

But then a voice rang out, shattering the difficult images that had succeeded in gaining entry into his head.

'Inspector? Forensics are done. They're ready for us.'

Chapter Three

He's definitely an odd sort, concluded Detective Sergeant Harry Thorne, as he smiled and waved Detective Inspector Sloane over to where he stood.

For a start, why has he taken so long to get here? I was down here like a shot. Soon as I got the tip-off. Couldn't find him anywhere.

DS Thorne had never worked with Detective Inspector Sloane before. No one he knew had ever worked with Detective Inspector Sloane before. He knew very little about him, just that he was originally from the area but had been up in some obscure place in the Midlands for years, and had now returned home.

When they had been introduced the previous day, DS Thorne had tried to break the ice. 'My name's Harry, but you can call me H,' he had quipped after the more formal introductions. The young sergeant had not yet worked out whether the absence of a smile in response was due to a lack of amusement, a lack of understanding, or just plain rudeness. Presumably they had televisions in the Birmingham area?

'Did you find it alright, Sir?' he enquired cautiously, as the Inspector approached.

'Yes, thanks. Was out on an errand earlier. I heard you'd gone on ahead. Have you been here long?' DI Sloane's tone was neutral, hard for the younger man to read.

'About half an hour or so. Been with the Forensics guys. They checked out here first. Nothing in the actual church so far that seems to suggest this was part of the actual crime scene. As you can imagine, the surfaces out here are going to be nothing but a mass of fingerprints and DNA. There were a few fresh sunflower petals on one of the front pews that didn't seem to match anything currently on display in the church. Could be something or nothing. They've focused their efforts on this little room where the body was discovered. No blood spotted anywhere else for now, so it looks like that's where it all went down.'

Sloane responded momentarily with an impassive stare.

'Would you like to lead the way? Oh, and next time, let's coordinate our arrivals at a crime scene, okay?'

DI Sloane knew how to reach the sacristy. But he quietly followed DS Thorne, observing him all the while. He was probably in his early thirties, and seemingly prone to an excessive use of aftershave and hair gel. The young sergeant wore his cheap, shiny suit with confidence and naivety in equal measure, his walk more a jaunty stroll than a deferential step. He had a foolish air of self-importance as he found himself guiding his superior to the crime scene, his enthusiasm and excitement utterly at odds with the bleakness of the scene that they would encounter. The older man knew they were a mismatch, a cliché; the tortured older detective and his cocky sidekick, still a bit wet round the ears, but with moments of brilliance, their initial suspicions destined to evolve into begrudging, mutual admiration. Or maybe not.

Right now, the Inspector had neither the energy nor the inclination to play out some hackneyed, formulaic, feel-good scenario. And he doubted very much that DS Harry Thorne would be able to fulfil his side of the bargain anyway.

Sloane knew that they were almost at the sacristy.

'Thorne,' he almost whispered, more due to trepidation than a need for confidentiality, as he abruptly came to a halt.

7

'Who exactly has been in that room, and who is in there at the moment?'

'Well, Forensics will still be in there packing up. Haven't seen them come out. Uniform arrived earlier, just after me, but I got them outside the church pretty much straight away to get the whole building taped off and then make sure no one else came in. I hope you didn't have any problems entering the building, Sir?'

Sloane wondered whether this was an attempt at humour or a bid to undermine his authority.

'What about the person who discovered the body?' he continued, ignoring the question, whatever its purpose had been.

'Right,' said Thorne, chirpily. 'So, I took an initial statement from her. Pretty shook up, she was.'

Shaken, thought Sloane, as Thorne, with undue ceremony, consulted his notepad.

'The lady's name was Maria Fernandez. She was here to do some cleaning, and had popped her head in to say good morning to the priest, our victim. To be honest, Sir, she was in a bit of a state, and it was hard to get much more than that out of her. It was Mrs Fernandez who alerted the emergency services, and she was the only person present when we turned up.'

'Right, we'll need to speak to her again as soon as possible. Have her fingerprints been taken?'

'Yes, Forensics did it before she was taken home. But with all due respect, Sir, she was a fairly elderly lady, around five foot tall, I'd say, armed with nothing more than a duster and furniture polish. I'm not sure that she's our prime suspect.'

While Thorne delighted in his amusing description, Sloane merely cringed. He took a deep breath and turned towards the nearby closed door. As he watched it, a beam of light, growing ever wider, poured out into the unlit corridor. He squinted, rooted to the spot, as two white-clad figures emerged.

Forensics, of course, he noted wryly, with a swift shake of his head. No ghosts of altar boys past, no celestial visions here. Definitely not. Just a scene of horror that would be all too real.

Sloane cleared his throat and addressed the two pairs of eyes just visible above paper masks, their expressions professional and detached.

'Afternoon,' he managed. There was no shakiness in his voice. But they couldn't see his hands, clasped deliberately behind his back.

Those eyes became warm, creasing with smiles.

'Inspector, good to see you. It's been a long time. How are you?' asked the older of the pathologists.

'David. Hello. Yes, fine thanks,' replied Sloane, equally warmly, though perhaps a little dismissively. 'So, any initial thoughts?' he continued. 'The cause of death? Time of death?'

'Well, cause of death seems to be due to a stabbing, sometime this morning with what appears to be a letter-opener. Blood loss would have followed, and with the victim not being discovered until lunchtime, death would have been inevitable.'

From behind him, Thorne's voice startled Sloane, as the young man smugly started to reel off a few further nuggets of information acquired earlier, 'The victim was the parish priest here at St Anthony's church, according to Mrs Fernandez. She said that there had been a weekday Mass here this morning. Mrs Fernandez was in attendance, but had then returned home for a while as her cat has been unwell.'

'Thank you, Sergeant,' replied Sloane evenly, noting the bristling of his colleagues in Forensics. 'Obviously we will need to speak to everyone who attended this morning's service. We shouldn't have to travel too far to track them down with any luck. Presumably they'll all live in the Haddelton area. For now, let's have a look at this room and our murder victim. Hopefully for us, the murderer left behind a couple of clues, forensic or otherwise, when they fled this crime scene. They often do.'

David raised his eyebrows meaningfully. Removing his mask now, he was able to speak more freely.

'We've brushed the whole room for fingerprints and have photographed everything. Obviously, the autopsy and toxicology reports will provide us with all the details on exactly how the victim died. However, why he died may certainly have something to do with what looks like an eye spray-painted onto one of the walls in there. We've taken scrapings to analyse. With any luck, this could get you a lead on what precisely was used and where it was bought.

Apart from that, the room seems to consist of the usual array of religious paraphernalia. Plenty of potential blunt instruments – heavy silver plates and chalices, weighty crucifixes, a couple of very solid statues, none of which appear to have been used in the attack, or as a defence. Apart from one storage cupboard and some shelving, the room is fairly sparsely furnished. There are a couple of clothes rails for various robes, and a table at the centre of the room with a few hymn books and some church leaflets on it. There's also a rota for church cleaning and flower arranging with a few names on it. Could be a good place to start as there appears to be nothing else of personal relevance in there? There's certainly no landline phone, and no mobile phone was found on or near the victim, or anywhere in the room for that matter. The poor man most likely suffered a slow, painful death, shut away in this bleak little room with no means of calling for help.'

Sloane observed the momentary compassion in this consummate professional, and turned briskly towards the open doorway. He knew exactly what he would see – the paradox of limbs clothed, adorned with sporadic items of jewellery, fingernails and hair with a lifetime of incorrigible persistence behind them, all now lying dormant, redundant, almost frivolous in their incongruity. He felt the older pathologist's eyes upon him as his gaze lingered on the lifeless body.

'Obviously we will all be able to get a whole lot more background information from his house next door. We'll keep you posted,' David assured him, as the pathologists turned to take their leave. He hesitated before calling back to him, 'It was good to see you, Robert.'

The ominous silence that ensued as the two detectives stood in the doorway, surveying the horror that met them, was broken eventually by Thorne. 'Have a look at the wall, Sir,' he suggested, with the slightly pompous air of someone taking pride in their prior knowledge. Riled, Sloane dragged his attention from the pitiful corpse before him and moved tentatively into the brightly-lit room. He could smell the paint immediately. It was pungent, like varnish.

'Quite strong, isn't it, Sir? If the stabbing didn't finish him off, maybe the fumes did,' laughed Thorne.

Sloane didn't even appear to hear him as he stared up at the sweeping black lines, arcs of swift movement, with a hastily drawn circle at their centre.

11

'Do you reckon someone was watching him, had their eye on him, so to speak?'

This time Sloane responded, still gazing up at the wall. 'In our job, we spend a lot of our time dealing with the need for compensation and justice. But, if we dig beneath the surface, isn't it really just the law of retaliation, the need to get even? Isn't that what's driving people, what drives all of us when we are wronged?'

He turned to look at his young colleague. 'An eye for an eye, Thorne. This could be an act of revenge. Pure revenge.'

For the first time that day, DS Thorne felt a disconcerting sense of unease. 'Well, lots of food for thought, so to speak,' he replied hesitantly. 'Shall we grab that rota? There might be a few old biddies on there that can fill in a few details for us.'

With one final, searching look around the room, Sloane nodded. 'Yes. The body can be released now for further investigation. Get someone from Uniform on this door until that happens.'

DI Sloane never went anywhere without a pair of the plastic gloves these days. Forensics had enough on their plate without having to eliminate his fingerprints every time he visited a crime scene. As he slipped the blue gloves on, he noticed for the first time that Thorne had been wearing his all along.

Picking up the rota with the short list of names scribbled onto it, the Inspector scanned the table at the centre of the room, leafing through the Mass sheets and hymn books. As he turned to leave, he quietly removed one of the Mass sheets, adding it to the transparent evidence wallet he'd produced from his pocket. It appeared to be the only other source of any information for now. Apart from this, the table was completely bare.

Chapter Four

Luca frowned, gazing unseeingly out across the terracotta rooftops concealing the steep, narrow lanes and steps. The evening sun still warmed the dusty pink medieval buildings, now a deep, vibrant orange, contrasting with the verdant, wooded slopes of Monte Subasio all around, so typical of the countryside in Umbria, that green heart of Italy.

Luca was due to leave Assisi tomorrow. The invitation had been unexpected, but perfectly timed. The alternative unbearable. He had sensed a certain urgency, and possibly even a little subterfuge, but everyone here had been in total agreement that it would be an invaluable opportunity, however curious the circumstances.

He had bidden farewell to his friends here, probably enjoying a little too much of the *Sagrantino*, the wonderful, local wine that he was unlikely to be tasting for the next couple of months. His parents had visited to wish him well. His father had fretted; his mother not so much.

He had managed, at very short notice, to secure a well-priced ticket to London from a local airport. Okay, the local airport wasn't actually in Umbria, and Stansted airport wasn't really that near to London. But that could be overlooked. It was all doable. The problem was that this was a non-transferable ticket, and his prospective host had suddenly become very elusive.

Luca had wanted to have that final call, a chance to run through the sketchy plans for the summer one more time. There had been plenty of communication since the invitation came in, but it had been for such a short amount of time. He still had so many questions.

As suppressed doubts continued to surface, he tried calling yet again. His stomach lurched as he heard the phone ring off, as it had done so many times that day, and with no option to leave a message.

Turning to look at his unusually tidy room, his packed bag sitting ready near the door, his phone charging, an alarm already set for his early morning start, Luca sighed. Outside, a solitary cloud passed in front of the sun and he shivered.

But it was at this moment that Luca decided two things. Firstly, he was going to find a landline number to leave a message on. Secondly, whether he was still welcome or not, he was getting on that flight to London tomorrow morning.

Chapter Five

THURSDAY

The green marker pen could be heard squeaking loudly in the silence of the meeting room, as DI Sloane slowly wrote the name Father Joseph Boletti at the centre of the large whiteboard commanding the attention of the gathered police officers and detectives. Photographs of the deceased were lying on the table in front of him, one of which he attached to the board beneath the victim's name, adjusting it until he was satisfied with its position.

Eventually, he turned to address the assembled Murder Investigation Team. Their eyes unwittingly exposed their wariness and uncertainty. Their expressions were guarded, circumspect. Sloane knew that he was an unknown quantity, an enigma, and that they were all reserving judgement on the Detective Inspector leading this case.

Yet he remained unperturbed. He'd seen it all before. Whatever their thoughts were about him, he sensed the intrigue and fascination. He recognised the curiosity. Not about him. But about the case. And he knew that, whatever their reservations were about him, that instinct to join the dots, to unravel a mystery, would keep this group of officers motivated. They'd all want to crack this case. Despite him.

Sloane cleared his throat. 'Morning. As most of you will know, I am Detective Inspector Sloane and I will be the Senior Investigating Officer on this case. Yesterday, the body of one Father Joseph Boletti, a Catholic priest, was found on the premises of his church with a stab wound to his abdomen. The church is St Anthony's Church in Briar Avenue, Haddelton. Obviously, not a million miles away from us here at the station. Forensics are currently carrying out the autopsy and will also provide toxicology reports. In the meantime, we will follow up a number of lines of enquiry.'

He picked up a piece of paper near him and carefully copied three names from it onto the board: Elizabeth Thompson, Maggie Gillingham, and Katie Evans. Then, almost with a flourish, he linked them to the victim's name with a long, green line.

'These three ladies were all signed up to a rota to help with church flowers and cleaning. They are unlikely to be our prime suspects, though obviously we can rule nothing out at this stage. But they may prove to be a useful source of information, with a lot of inside knowledge of the dynamic of this parish, possibly going back years, if not decades. We need to track down and speak to all of them, separately, as quickly as possible. Let's try not to intimidate them though. They are probably going to be significantly distressed at the news.'

Sloane then added the name Maria Fernandez with its own line running to the priest's name.

'This lady discovered the body. Detective Sergeant Thorne spoke to her at the time.'

Reluctantly, the Inspector gestured for DS Thorne to relay all that he had gauged from the distraught parishioner, anticipating a few moments of cringeworthy self-importance. Instead, Sloane noted a certain awkwardness as Thorne read out his notes. If anything, the young sergeant appeared overly earnest, his eyes darting towards him at times, either for approval or reassurance, or as though he were out of his depth in something and was struggling with how to play it. It was impossible to tell.

The Inspector nodded his thanks noncommittally.

'Thorne and I will be paying Mrs Fernandez a visit immediately after this briefing,' he announced. 'I have already managed to speak to the local bishop, who was understandably extremely shocked to hear of the events of yesterday. He confirmed that Father Joseph had been the parish priest at St Anthony's for over twenty years, and was well-loved by all accounts. Prior to that, he remembered he'd been based in Kent for around ten years. We'll need someone to chase up details of his time over there. Somewhere near Tunbridge Wells, I think. Something could have resurfaced after all these years. You never know.

Obviously, with a surname like Boletti, there was clearly a connection to another country, presumably Italy, somewhere along the line. We'll need to do a bit of digging here. We may need to go right back to his childhood. Find out where he was born. What was his family background? Was Joseph his original name? If not, was there a reason he's been going by the name of Father Joseph all these years? Why did he become a priest? Why did he end up living abroad in safe, leafy neighbourhoods, dressed like thousands of other men of the cloth?

The bishop I spoke to is going to do some digging of his own, but as of this morning, he could not think of one reason why anybody would contemplate harming, let alone murdering, this long-serving clergyman, happily ensconced at the centre of the local Catholic community, with no plans to move on or retire any time soon. He was adamant that it must have been a random attack, an attempted burglary gone wrong. However, he is as yet unaware of the drawing of the eye on the wall.'

At this point, Sloane reached for a photograph of the eye and attached it to the board. 'As you will have heard, for some reason, a design resembling an eye was left on the wall of the sacristy where the body was found. Any suggestions or leads regarding the relevance of this could be pivotal in this enquiry. Quite why someone would choose to take the time to spray a large clue to the reason they carried out a murder is somewhat unfathomable from where I'm standing.

That is, of course, if it were the perpetrator. Unlikely I know, but could it have been the victim attempting to expose his assassin? There was no sign of any spray can in the room, but Forensics are looking into the type of paint used, so we may get a lead on where it could have been sourced. Whoever did this, clearly had a message to get across. Just what was that message? Had Father Joseph been under surveillance? Was his murder an act of revenge?'

DI Sloane scowled suddenly as a loud, insistent knock on the door interrupted him. A young police officer, clearly uncomfortable, appeared in the open doorway, holding out in front of him a piece of hastily torn-off paper. 'Apologies, Inspector,' he almost croaked, 'A Forensics team have been combing through the victim's home next door to the church. There were a couple of messages on a landline phone they found, the first of which could be pretty significant.'

Faltering under the weight of the room's attention, he moved hesitantly to hand on the note in his possession. Sloane, already striding towards him, relieved him of it gratifyingly swiftly.

Sloane's brow creased as he took in what he read.

'Well, in my book, there is no such thing as a coincidence,' he announced emphatically as he looked up.

'According to a message left on the victim's landline phone yesterday, an unknown male, going by the name of Luca - another Italian I assume - is due to arrive later today as an invited guest.' He paused. 'Yet approximately twenty-four hours before his arrival, his host is brutally murdered. I would be very surprised if there wasn't a connection here.'

He turned and wrote the name Luca, with its own heavy line drawn towards the victim's name. 'Someone else we clearly need to talk to. Pick him up as soon as he arrives at the church premises.'

DS Thorne, listening intently, was then almost blindsided as Sloane turned to him and asked, 'How's your Spanish, Thorne? We're off to see Mrs Fernandez.'

Utterly unable to determine whether this was an attempt at humour or a genuine question, he responded feebly with a half-hearted *olé* and pulled on his jacket.

Chapter Six

'Ladies and Gentlemen, we have begun our descent into London Stansted. Please turn off all portable electronic devices and stow them until we have arrived at the gate.'

As the announcement continued, Luca peered out at the patchwork of fields below him, all neatly cultivated, a healthy, deep green, sewn together with the ribbons of foliage criss-crossing them raggedly. They had just emerged beneath the thick, grey cloud that had been disconcertingly rattling the plane for the last few minutes. A mere two-hour journey, yet long gone were the vivid blue skies; the heat that shimmered above the tarmac of the deserted runway at Ancona airport; the parched, rustic landscape, replaced almost immediately on take-off by its equally glorious antithesis, the rippled, turquoise expanse of the Adriatic Sea.

Luca glanced at his fellow passengers, predominantly Italians. The stylish sunglasses; the fitted t-shirts, unforgiving, although there was generally little to forgive, serving in reality to display prized suntans; the expensive, leather sandals revealing perfectly painted toenails. All worn with practised nonchalance at the departure gate. All redundant now, incongruous in the impending Essex drizzle. Most of it now reluctantly concealed under more weatherproof, less flattering items of clothing. Glamour would prove to be far more challenging in these British climes, Luca noted, zipping up his over-sized fleece. The dark jacket engulfed his slender frame. His fair hair, pleasingly unkempt, no longer caught the sunlight; his eyes, normally a bright blue, reflected only hues of silver. Even his olive complexion seemed to pale, revealing the endearing smattering of freckles on his slightly upturned nose.

Spontaneous outbursts of applause from Italian occupied pockets of the cabin accompanied the smooth, uneventful landing. The subsequent disembarkation involved a somewhat chaotic, yet entirely good-natured, lack of queueing or order. All met, naturally, with indulgent tolerance by the returning British holidaymakers, still replete, rested and relaxed, still a little in love with Italy.

Luca, dispirited, in notable contrast to the anticipation surrounding him, switched his phone back on as he waited at the carousel currently churning out the flight's luggage. The lack of any communication was really starting to concern him now. He had received no response after leaving that message on the landline number yesterday evening. He had realised this morning that stupidly he hadn't left his contact details. But, surely, they already had his mobile number? His heart sank all the more as he peered down at his frustratingly empty phone screen.

The more imaginative amongst us might term it as a premonition, the more pragmatic preferring to define it as a logical conclusion. But Luca felt in that particular moment that this foray into uncharted territory would prove to be more challenging and complicated than he could ever have anticipated.

He sighed, lunging for his paltry worldly belongings, encased within a soft black holdall of striking similarity to a significant number presently circling, and headed for the train station. Luca had travelled to England on many occasions, but never to this part of London, and never in this capacity.

Chapter Seven

The neat, end-of-terrace Victorian house belonging to Maria Fernandez was, perhaps unsurprisingly, very close to St Anthony's church. It sat at the beginning of a quiet, well-kept cul-de-sac. The cars parked along both sides of the road created a sense of cramped narrowness that did not do the pretty road justice. The vehicles almost obscured the attractive facades with their smart doorways painted in various shades of grey and sage green, the smooth black and white tiled pathways that led to them, and the brightly coloured, potted geraniums dotted around the compact front gardens, supposedly with insouciance; in reality with the precision of a master draughtsman.

With no doorbell in sight, DS Thorne was not sure whether to knock gently or decisively. He could sense that DI Sloane was watching his every move. And it was making him nervous. Very nervous. He was spared any attempt at a 'brisk but friendly' approach, when the door unexpectedly opened, revealing a tired, lined face, etched with concern and fear.

But, confusingly, it was not the face of the lady he had briefly spoken to the previous day.

'Afternoon. I'm Detective Sergeant Thorne, and this is Detective Inspector Sloane. We were hoping to speak to Mrs Maria Fernandez,' said Thorne, reading out the name a little haltingly as he consulted his notepad.

'Come in. I'm Doreen. I live next door,' the woman explained.

She shuffled back along the narrow hallway, and led the two men into a small living-room at the front of the house.

A large bay window dominated the cosy space, and daylight flooded in, silhouetting the figure seated on the sofa nestled against it. As she raised her tear-stained face to meet their gaze, DI Sloane, caught momentarily off-guard, felt himself metaphorically ripping up the profile description provided by DS Thorne.

This lady was not elderly. In her fifties, certainly. But with her glamorous, dark looks and ageless elegance, her advancing years only worked to her advantage; they only served to enhance her attributes. As for being barely five foot tall, it was hard to tell. However, far from seeming diminutive in stature, she had a large, vibrant presence. Sloane would describe her as voluptuous. But he would wisely refrain from including that adjective in any resulting reports.

'Mrs Fernandez?' clarified Sloane from where he stood. Doreen had taken the only armchair in the room, and he and Thorne could hardly squeeze in either side of this tearful lady, all sinking into each other amongst her scatter cushions.

'It's Miss Fernandez, actually,' came the snuffled response.

Sloane observed her as the full, dark lashes that framed her large, brown eyes batted away any remaining tears in an alarmingly attractive fashion.

'Miss Fernandez,' he continued, mustering all the professionalism he could, 'We understand that this must be a distressing time for you, but we need to ask you a few more questions.'

Maria nodded slowly, her lustrous black hair falling gently across her face.

'Why did you enter the sacristy yesterday lunchtime? In your chat with my colleague yesterday, you stated that you

23

were there to clean the church. We have a copy of a rota for flowers and cleaning. Your name is not on it for Wednesdays. Or any other day of the week for that matter.'

The two detectives looked at Maria expectantly.

'I was there to clean,' she replied with a sigh. 'The reason that I am not on the rota is that I always do Wednesdays. I have done for years. And everyone else just works around that.'

'How many years exactly have you been doing this?'

'Eighteen. Since I moved from Spain to this country.'

'Can I ask if you attended Mass yesterday morning?'

'Yes, I did. I think I confirmed this with your colleague yesterday. I tend to go whenever I can. It is often just a very small group of us. Seven or eight people at times.'

'We will need you to provide information on anyone who was present yesterday if you can. Can I ask if you or anyone else brought fresh flowers into the church yesterday?'

'I don't tend to deal with the flowers really, and I didn't notice anyone with flowers yesterday. I can try to give you some names certainly.'

'We understand you went home after the Mass, returning to the church sometime later?'

'That is correct. My cat, Fifi, has been a little poorly lately and I needed to check on her.'

As if on cue, a large, sleek, black cat sauntered past the two detectives, glancing at them with utter indifference.

'I'm sorry to hear that. How is, er, Fifi now?' replied Sloane, taking in the well-fed feline rubbing contentedly at Doreen's legs, a picture of health.

'So much better now, thankfully,' smiled Maria, tilting her head to gaze adoringly at her miraculously recovered cat.

Sloane raised his eyebrows.

'Miss Fernandez, you have obviously been a member of this parish for quite some time. Can you think of any reason why someone would have wanted to harm Father Joseph?'

Instead of replying, Maria's eyes welled up and she let out a woeful howl.

Sloane wondered if this display of unparalleled grief was the result of a Mediterranean temperament or an undiscovered talent for amateur dramatics. He glanced at Thorne, whose eyes betrayed a scepticism that matched his own.

Doreen leant across to Maria with more tissues and then turned her attention to the two detectives, both now oscillating between sympathy and cynicism. Veering significantly towards the cynicism, if the truth be told.

'Maria is obviously very distressed about what has happened, not a stone's throw from our door. It's all very worrying. If she can think of anything else that might help you with your enquiries, I am sure she will let you know. Won't you Maria?'

Maria nodded, her face buried in the palms of her hands.

'Now, I have to get back to check on a casserole I'm making for us. I'll show you gentlemen out as I leave.'

With that, she stood up and gestured to the door. Sloane took one last glance around the room. It was charming, he had to concede, all centred around a small, Victorian, cast-iron fireplace, with dried flowers and pillar candles artfully positioned in its hearth. A deep pink Persian rug covered much of the room's weathered, wooden floor, complementing the elegant sofa and thick, full-length curtains that framed the bay window. A dark bookshelf took up the space on one side of the fireplace, housing a few rows of neat paperbacks in both English and Spanish. To the other side, a small television and a music system were slotted in, a pile of DVDs and CDs stacked neatly next to them. It was all very homely and tasteful. All pretty normal really.

Sloane recognised the vivid, abstract, framed prints on one wall. A nod to her Spanish heritage, he guessed. A little quirky maybe, but not exactly damning evidence. He did note, however, that there were no photos on display in the room. But again, it was very little to go on. How did the evil or insane choose to furnish their homes, he mused? What was a murderer's house supposed to look like?

'We'll be in touch, Miss Fernandez,' he said, with one final glance at the perfectly plumped up cushions on Maria's sofa.

Outside the house, the two men remained silent, their expressions neutral until Doreen was safely behind her closed front door and they were inside their vehicle. As Thorne started up the car, he turned to Sloane, inappropriate mirth written all over his face. Sloane caught his eye and, despite himself, broke out into a wide grin.

They were still smiling as they nodded at the patrol car stationed near the church, acknowledging the two police officers who would shortly be intercepting the solitary stranger inspecting the police tape that ominously crossed the door of St Anthony's church.

From her bay window, Maria silently watched the detectives and her neighbour leave. Discarding her wet tissues, she turned and headed over to her bookshelf, pulling out her favourite book of all. It fell open easily in her hands, and the glossy photographs that lay between its pages caught the light as she stared down at them. She, too, smiled.

Chapter Eight

In a nearby coffee house, Elizabeth, Maggie and Katie sat huddled together in front of their untouched hot drinks. All around them, people chatted in a relaxed manner, and carefree laughs punctuated the casual conversations taking place at the compact round tables, a small posy of fresh flowers at their centre. The tables were never quite large enough to house the wide mugs of cappuccino and overly generous portions of homemade cake served there. Though no one quite had the appetite for cake that morning.

'Do you think we are going to be prime suspects? Our fingerprints must be everywhere.' Elizabeth tore impatiently at a small packet of sugar as she spoke.

'Shush, be careful,' replied Maggie in a whisper, looking guardedly over both shoulders. 'There are police everywhere at the moment. There is still a police car outside the church today apparently. I haven't been past, as it might look a little odd, to say the least.'

'I think we definitely need to think about alibis,' continued Elizabeth with a steely focus. 'What were we all doing yesterday morning? Let's make sure we are all clear on everyone's movements, and then we can corroborate each other's stories if need be. Do you think they will take mugshots of us? Oh God, they are always so awful.'

Katie laid her hands on the table firmly, coffee slopping from their mugs into awaiting saucers. They always managed to pick a table with legs that weren't quite level.

'Ladies, ladies, let's calm down here. Just because we are kind enough to help with the church flowers and do a bit of cleaning, not to mention the admin I've been doing recently, doesn't mean we killed our parish priest.'

'Means, motive and opportunity. That's what they will be looking for,' countered Maggie. 'We may have had the means and the opportunity, but what possible motive could we have for doing something like this? I just don't see how they would be able to pin it on us.'

'Heaven knows what Maria will say. I wouldn't put it past her to imply something incriminating,' sighed Elizabeth.

But Maggie wasn't listening. She was looking at Katie. 'What admin have you been doing, Katie? I didn't know you'd been doing anything like that.'

'Oh, nothing much. Just helping with some accounting and phone calls, stuff like that,' replied Katie breezily, as she busily checked her watch. 'Ladies, drink up, it's nearly three o'clock. We'd better head up to school.'

Katie watched as Maggie and Elizabeth headed for the counter, waving their platinum bank cards around, both vying to pay for the coffees. Maggie, always impeccably groomed at the school gate, wore her impossibly white jeans and tailored linen jacket with her usual aplomb. Her elegance and poise, combined with a fierce intelligence, had rendered her utterly intimidating initially. Yet this seemingly formidable figure had taken Katie under her wing; she had been a guiding light in this unfamiliar territory.

Maggie was long accustomed to wealth, unlike Elizabeth, who had spent many years in the wilderness before a dramatic change in fortune, from which she had never looked back. Meeting and marrying Greg, and having her younger son, Tom, with him, all in the last few years, had transformed her from a struggling single mother to an

28

affluent lady-who-lunches with an expensive gym membership. As usual, Elizabeth was clad today in high-quality sportswear, her sleek, blonde hair tied back in a ponytail at the perfect angle. She coordinated their coffees and lunches with her Pilates and yoga classes.

Both in their late thirties, neither of these women's figures betrayed their motherhood. Yet they each had two children, the younger ones serving as the glue that had bonded them and Katie.

All three of their children had been placed in the same class when they had started school nearly two years ago. Katie had not known a soul back then, and had tentatively welcomed the advice, borne of experience, offered by these two women. In spite of her reservations, and her slightly younger age – Katie had still been in her twenties when she'd met them - she had embraced the camaraderie they offered; their wry humour had definitely helped as she negotiated Primary school life; from PE kit and spelling test reminders to dress-up days and collections for the teachers, Maggie and Elizabeth knew the game. This was second time around for them. They had become unlikely allies, and Katie had avoided many a pitfall thanks to them.

Now at the doorway, Katie watched her friends as they picked their way between the tables, presumably trying to look as inconspicuous as possible, but failing miserably. She could only imagine their Instagram posts. All blue skies, big smiles and #livingmybestlife captions.

Needing to keep a low profile, Katie had to avoid all the social media websites. It was anonymity she craved. A clean slate. A fresh start. For herself. And for Alex. Turning six soon, he barely remembered their former life. He no longer asked after the missing jigsaw pieces from his earliest years.

29

Pushing open the door of the café, Katie looked up at the leaden sky. 'I wonder how Greek Day went in Year One. Shame they didn't have Greek weather. And it's meant to be so nice from tomorrow. Finally going to feel like summer with any luck. We really need some sunshine – May's been an absolute wash-out. Anyway, hopefully they got outside for their Greek picnic. Pitta bread and humous all round, I think. Goodness knows what state their togas are going to be in.'

Maggie laughed. 'Noah's cost a fortune too. I couldn't work out how to muddle one out of a sheet. Life's too short.'

Katie saw Maggie's eyes cloud with regret at her choice of words. She and Elizabeth exchanged glances.

'Well, I'm glad they didn't cancel the whole thing after what's happened,' mustered Elizabeth. 'The children are all going to be so upset and confused. They definitely need as much routine and normality as possible.'

The three friends continued their short walk to the school in a contemplative silence, which was strangely as far removed from their own routine and normality as was possible.

Chapter Nine

'He's what?!' cried Luca.

The interview room was bare, apart from the large table that lay between the young man and the two detectives sitting opposite him, open files containing notes and photographs in front of them.

'Yes, unfortunately Father Joseph Boletti was discovered dead yesterday lunchtime. And today you have arrived. We would like you to talk us through exactly what you are doing here, Mr…?'

'Rossetti. Luca Rossetti.'

Sloane turned towards the tape recorder that sat at one end of the table. 'For the record, Mr Rossetti has been offered legal representation but has declined.'

'Can I just get this straight?' Luca continued, a disbelieving, panicked tone to his voice. 'Father Joseph died yesterday – someone I had never spoken to before last week – and now you are interviewing me under caution as a possible accomplice to his murder?'

'Yes,' came the brief reply.

Luca dragged his fingers through his mop of fair hair and held his head in despair. His golden skin was now flushed red, and dark rings were forming beneath his uneasy eyes.

'Listen, you do know that there is a global shortage of Catholic priests these days? Do you really think I would have to arrange for a priest to be bumped off to get a position for the summer?'

Luca was now gesticulating wildly.

'A position for the summer?' Sloane repeated with some incredulity. 'Doing what exactly?'

'Well, we hadn't discussed it in great depth.'

'We?'

'Father Joseph and myself.'

Thorne, all ears, cleared his throat.

'How long were you planning on staying for?'

'Just a couple of months until my studies start again in September. I did something similar last summer, but that was in Italy.'

Sloane and Thorne exchanged glances.

'Look, this is ridiculous," shouted Luca, as he unzipped his fleece, peeled it off and flung it onto the chair beside him.

Sloane narrowed his eyes. Thorne choked on the coffee he was sipping.

'Now what?' asked Luca, incensed.

'You didn't think to mention you were a priest?' Sloane asked, turning once again to the tape recorder. 'For the record, Mr Rossetti is wearing a black shirt with a clerical white collar.'

'Well, why else would I be here? Actually… I'm not a priest. Well, I am, sort of…'

Sloane took a deep breath. 'I think you need to start at the beginning, Mr Rossetti. Take your time.'

The potentially perilous nature of his predicament was not lost on Luca. In front of him sat two English detectives, staring intently at him, awaiting an explanation for this seemingly curious set of circumstances. A man had been murdered, someone whom he knew very little about, who had invited him into his life at very short notice. What had he become embroiled in here? Was he about to be framed for involvement in a murder that he had nothing to do with, unable to prove his innocence, circumstantial evidence condemning him beyond all reasonable doubt? The panic that gripped him had been insidious, creeping up on him stealthily. But he was all too aware of it now. His head hummed, his mouth was dry, his stomach churned, and his heart thumped against his ribs like never before.

'Can we get you some water or a cup of coffee or tea?' asked the older detective, with a hint of kindness, it seemed.

'Yes, yes please,' Luca managed. 'Coffee would be great, thank you.'

As he waited for his much-needed drink, Luca contemplated what these detectives needed to know.

Luca had been born in Italy, near to Ancona, almost thirty years ago, the only child of a rather handsome local man and the English girl who'd fallen in love with him while working out there. So in love had she been, that she'd left behind the considerable delights of West Dorset to embrace life in the quaint little town in central Italy where her soon-to-be husband lived. Marriage to Luca's father was a decision that she had never come to regret. Regular visits to Dorset, where the beautiful Jurassic Coast surely rivalled the magic of the Conero Riviera on their doorstep in Italy, had ensured that Luca had known the love of her own parents while they were alive, and had, of course, spoken plenty of English.

The day that Luca had sat his parents down and explained to them that he planned to enter a seminary had been an arduous one. To say they were ill-disposed to the idea was a considerable understatement. Both nominally Catholic, neither profoundly devout, they were unyielding in their opposition. They had harboured dreams of an expanding family, lively grandchildren to busy themselves with, Luca and his beautiful wife grateful for all their support. It was incomprehensible to them why a young man in his prime, with a university degree already under his belt, not to mention the sweet girlfriend he had loved for too many years to remember, would want to deny himself all the adventures that life could bring. It wasn't as if Luca had ever been particularly religious. His mother blamed it on the Philosophy he had studied at university.

'What about poor Giulia?' they had asked, concerned for the delightful girl who had spent so many years at Luca's side. It was only when Luca explained that 'poor' Giulia was busy planning not only a wedding, but also a christening, clearly not involving him, that his parents had understood.

It had been a broken heart that had led Luca to the splendid buildings of the seminary in Assisi. Looming over the leafy valley beneath it, all Romanesque arches and private courtyards, the Friary that Luca now called home was attached to the town's Basilica. The Basilica where St Francis, the local saint, famed for being so enamoured of the beauty of nature, now lay interred in a cold, stone crypt. How apt, his parents had thought.

While Luca had embraced whole-heartedly his sudden vocation, and saw the warm, stone architecture with its glorious frescoes and porticos as a spiritual refuge, his parents saw only a fortress in which he had imprisoned himself.

Luca was to spend four years studying here, each summer being assigned to a different parish to assist with ministerial duties. Last summer, at the end of his first year, he had been fortunate enough to be placed in a parish local to Assisi for two months. This year, however, there was a very real prospect that his summer would be spent back in his home parish. Even his parents, filled with joy at the very idea, knew that this would be an excruciating ordeal for their wretched son, for whom it would be impossible to avoid the young girl who had so casually flung him aside, and who was now taking such pleasure in marriage and motherhood.

How serendipitous, therefore, that a need had arisen, further away from Ancona than Luca could ever have hoped for. He was, of course, the perfect candidate. His mother had only ever spoken to him in her native tongue, so his English was perfect, accent free.

Nevertheless, his peers, unaware of the circumstances of his calling, were a little taken aback at the vigour of his enthusiasm when the unconventional request had come in.

A former seminarian, whose occasional visits had ensured an enduring bond despite his many years away, Father Giuseppe Boletti had provided the answer to all Luca's desperate prayers. With full approval from the seminary, Luca had embarked on a week of excited phone calls and hasty travel arrangements. Father Joseph, as he now referred to himself, didn't appear to want to burden the keen apprentice with too much detail, and seemed at pains that Luca should arrive as soon as he was able. However, he sounded amiable enough during their brief chats. He'd been laughingly concerned as to whether calls to Italy would be using up all the minutes on his phone contract. And he was certainly happy to host Luca at St Anthony's for two months until his studies resumed in September. Luca had decided not to overthink the situation. After all, what other options did he have?

DI Sloane and DS Thorne had sat in silence, listening to Luca without interruption as he provided his somewhat censored version of events. But now suddenly Sloane leaned forward. 'Can you clarify that Father Joseph was using a mobile phone to communicate with you?'

'Yes,' replied Luca, 'Well, until Wednesday when I ended up having to leave a message on a landline number. Presumably a message you are aware of, judging by the welcome committee outside the church earlier. Obviously, I know now why Father Joseph wasn't taking my calls. At least there should be some sort of record of me on his mobile phone which will back up my story.'

Sloane stayed silent. Despite extensive searches of the church and the victim's home, no mobile phone had been recovered. As he understood it, apart from Father Joseph, three people had entered the sacristy before Forensics began their work: the murderer, Maria Fernandez, and Detective Sergeant Thorne. He glanced sideways at the young officer who appeared to be busily consulting his notes.

The young sergeant looked up. 'So, just to clarify,' he enquired slowly, and perhaps a little patronisingly, 'You are training to be a priest, and are here in England for some work experience, due to your excellent knowledge of the English language?' He made no reference to the mobile phone.

Luca, who had decided not to bother the detectives with the details of the heartbreak that had been the catalyst for his current direction in life, nodded in relief.

But Sloane missed this. He was still watching Thorne, wondering whether his young colleague was one step behind in this game, or actually one step ahead.

A loud knock on the door of the interview room interrupted the Inspector's thoughts.

'A word, Sir,' came a voice as the door opened.

'I'll be right with you,' replied Sloane, as he turned to Luca. 'I want you to think of absolutely anything you can, anything that was said in your conversations, that might provide us with a clue as to why Father Joseph was murdered.' He nodded to Thorne, not quite meeting his eye, and left the room.

'Okay. So, his story checks out,' confirmed the waiting officer.

'Who did you speak to then?' asked Sloane.

'We got through to the seminary in Assisi. Not much English spoken there clearly, but enough to confirm that he's telling the truth. He's been living there for two years, and his visit to the UK is all above board as far as they're concerned.'

'Right. We'll just get him to make a statement then, and let him go. Still seems a bit of a coincidence to me though.'

'There was something else,' added the officer with a slight grimace.

'What? Sounds ominous,' demanded Sloane, clearly piqued.

'Well, we've been having to liaise with the bishop. And once he found out that Father Joseph had arranged for this young priest to come over from Italy, and that it was all hunky dory, well, he was basically over the moon. He's arranging for the young lad to stay with a neighbouring priest, and wants him to take over at St Anthony's for the time being, starting with a Mass on Sunday. He's trying to get someone permanent as quickly as possible. But in the meantime, and these are his words not mine, the show must go on.'

'For God's sake. What about preserving the crime scene? I don't believe this.'

'Well, I guess we can keep the sacristy cordoned off. To be honest, it's that young chap in there I feel sorry for. He might be about to find that he's bitten off a lot more than he can chew.'

Chapter Ten

FRIDAY

Katie had known the call would come sooner or later; an invitation to answer a few questions. Did her little more than tenuous links to St Anthony's church really warrant a police interview? Or had her non-existent online profile been a red flag? What sort of background checks were detectives able to carry out these days? Her relief had been palpable on hearing that Maggie and Elizabeth had also been contacted, their indignation obviously vying with terror, but both reactions clearly eclipsed by a furtive thrill about it all.

Katie was to meet a Detective Inspector Sloane in the church reception area for an informal chat at half past nine, the first of three separate appointments with The Flower Lady Three.

The day had dawned fine and warm, and she already felt uncomfortably hot in the clothes she had thrown on a little earlier that morning. The effort that went into school gate outfits still intimidated her, but had clearly not been a source of inspiration for her look today. In a thick, shapeless dress that concealed her petite frame, her unruly, auburn hair hurriedly scraped back in a bun, Katie had given little thought to the sartorial requirements of the day. During the frantic morning routine that had ensured Alex arrived at school fed, dressed, and with his reading book signed, Katie's mind had been elsewhere.

To her consternation, there were two officers, rather than one, waiting to speak to her when she entered the church foyer. Her colour rose in panic. She was out of breath, partly due to the rushed walk here from the school after a hushed conversation with Maggie and Elizabeth. She was also undeniably nervous.

'Katie Evans?' asked the older of the two men. 'I am Detective Inspector Sloane and this is my colleague, Detective Sergeant Thorne. Thank you for coming to talk to us. Would you like to take a seat? We'd just like to ask you a few questions regarding the death of Father Joseph.'

As Katie sat down reluctantly on a nearby chair, she noticed that the younger officer was already writing something in his notepad. Had she aroused suspicion already, she wondered?

'Firstly, we are sorry if this is all rather distressing for you. How well did you know Father Joseph?' continued the Inspector.

'Fairly well,' replied Katie shakily. 'I help out a bit with flowers. I've also been doing some admin recently. The person who'd been covering it all had retired after years of helping out, so Father Joseph was a bit stuck.'

'Can I ask if you attended the Mass here yesterday morning?'

'No, I didn't.'

'Can you confirm where you were up until lunchtime yesterday? Sorry, we have to ask these questions as part of a process of elimination.'

'Of course, of course.'

Katie tried not to sound as though she had rehearsed this a hundred times already. 'I took my son to school as usual and then went straight home as I had a bit of a headache. I'm so sorry but I was actually on my own for most of the day. Once my headache had cleared, I did a bit of cleaning of my flat and baked a few scones. I'm not great at baking but my son loves them. Sorry, that's probably not particularly relevant.' Katie laughed awkwardly. 'Anyway, I would say I could bring a scone in as evidence, but we've managed to get through them all between us. Again, not helpful, I guess. As I said, I was literally at home on my own for several hours. I don't remember speaking to anyone until later in the day. It was only when I went back to the school, just after three o'clock, that I first became aware there'd been an incident at the church. People had spotted the police cars and the cordons. You can imagine the rumours sweeping around the playground. The school sent out an email a little later. I can't tell you how shocked we all are.'

'Can you think of anyone who would have wanted to harm Father Joseph? Or any reason at all why his life would have been in danger?'

Katie shook her head miserably, suspecting that these two seasoned detectives had the ability to see into her very soul.

'Have you been in this parish for long?' asked DS Thorne, notepad poised, his pen worryingly ready for action.

'Nearly two years,' she replied. Katie knew what was coming next.

Yet, in that very moment, two figures loomed at the large glass door to the foyer, pushing it open and entering silently. Sloane turned, clearly irritated. 'This is still partly a crime scene. Could you pl…'

The Inspector's demeanour changed as he took in the two men standing there. 'Father O'Leary?' His intonation revealed his uncertainty.

'Robert. It's been a long time,' said the elderly priest.

There was a brief pause. Sloane stayed silent.

'Can I introduce Father Luca?' continued Father O'Leary, breaking the silence. 'He is kindly going to be taking on a few duties here at St Anthony's following the awful events of this week.'

'We've met,' laughed Father Luca, as he nodded to the two officers. 'I'm sorry, are we interrupting a meeting here?'

'It's fine. We were more or less done for now,' replied Sloane, seemingly keen to bring the interview to a close. 'In fact, Katie here might be just the person you'll want to talk to. She will have some knowledge of church affairs here at St Anthony's.'

'If that's okay with you, of course, Mrs Evans?' he checked, turning his attention back to Katie.

Katie nodded, although she wasn't actually looking at him. This was something she would immediately come to regret, as her eyes had instead been quietly travelling down the length of the young priest's legs and she was currently admiring his gorgeous suede desert boots. Men didn't often get footwear right. She was impressed. Now, with everyone else's eyes upon her, she suddenly felt a little caught out.

Fortunately for Katie, the young cleric appeared to remain entirely impervious to any curiosity on her part. Luca smiled warmly at her, his blue eyes crinkling charmingly, 'Mrs Evans, I would be grateful for any help you can offer.'

Katie wondered just how inappropriate it would be to correct him on her marital status at that moment in time.

'Absolutely, Father,' she replied. 'I can run through a few things now if that works for everybody?'

41

DI Sloane smiled gratefully, while DS Thorne snapped his notebook shut, perhaps a little theatrically.

'Actually, just one more question please, Mrs Evans?' Thorne asked suddenly.

Katie's heart sank, and not just because she was being referred to as Mrs Evans again.

'Did you bring any sunflowers into the church in the days leading up to Father Joseph's death?'

'Flowers are usually changed on a Friday, before the weekend Masses. So, no, definitely not. I know for a fact that none of us would have brought any flowers in before Friday,' confirmed Katie, extremely relieved to be answering flower related questions, sunflowers or otherwise.

Father O'Leary patted Sloane on the back as the two detectives rose to take their leave.

'Good to see you, Robert. You take care now,' he said.

But, by then, the Inspector was already outside, and the glass door had swung emphatically closed behind him.

Chapter Eleven

'Any thoughts on Mrs Katie Evans?' asked Sloane, as he slowly manoeuvred their car back towards the station.

Thorne had thoughts. He had a lot of thoughts. But they were not about Katie Evans. He could not have failed to notice the uneasy rapport between Sloane and that elderly priest. Rather than continuing to question a potentially vital witness to any scenario that may have unfolded at St Anthony's church, the Inspector had appeared anxious to bring their interview to a close as quickly as possible.

During their second inspection of the church and the crime scene that morning, Sloane had displayed a definite familiarity with the environment, yet a distinct discomfort. Thorne knew very little about this man's past, apart from the fact that he had moved away from here decades ago. What was the Inspector's connection with this church all those years ago? And what exactly had he been doing at the time of the murder of Father Joseph Boletti?

In the meantime, Thorne's interest in the flower lady angle had now dwindled rather considerably. 'I don't think Mrs Evans is our prime suspect to be honest. And neither are the other two we are supposed to be talking to later. And that's despite her lack of a solid alibi, and being about thirty years younger than I'd expected her to be. For someone potentially trying hard to cover her tracks after brutally murdering her parish priest, she did get a little too distracted by the appearance of our Mr Rossetti.'

'Some people just have less of a conscience than you or me, Thorne,' said Sloane, pulling smoothly into a parking bay at the station. 'Though she doesn't seem to have been in this parish very long. Nevertheless, these flower ladies might still be able to provide some background information as and when we need it. For now, let's see if anyone has dug up anything interesting back here.'

Chapter Twelve

Father O'Leary appeared perfectly happy to be leaving Father Luca in Katie's capable hands. He fretted briefly about him remembering the directions back to his own church, then headed off gratefully, albeit looking warily over his shoulder from time to time until he reached the safety of his car.

Still smiling from the elderly clergyman's well-meant fussing, Father Luca turned to look at Katie expectantly. Katie, who had pulled the hairband out of her hair and was trying to discreetly shake her head around to add some volume to her lacklustre locks - scolding herself all the while for her utterly inappropriate behaviour – returned the young, handsome priest's gaze with what, she hoped, was an expression of earnest welcome. She wasn't to know that her eyes instead betrayed a fascination that went way beyond the solemn circumstances of their business.

'So, Mrs Evans, was it?' he asked.

'It's Katie,' she replied, almost accidentally purring. 'And you are Father Luke?'

'It's Father Luca, actually. Just flown in from Italy, would you believe? I live out there, but my mother is English.'

Father Luca watched, confused, as this friendly English girl's face clouded over, her eyes becoming nervous and guarded.

'I hadn't realised. You don't look particularly Italian, and your English is perfect. Which part of Italy are you from?'

Father Luca could hear a tremor in her voice. She seemed to relax slightly as he replied, 'Near Ancona. But I live in Assisi these days. That's where I'm in a seminary.'

He wondered silently if he had put his foot in it already. Was he supposed to mention that he wasn't quite a fully-fledged priest yet? If he was honest, he was having grave doubts about this whole situation. He wasn't exactly qualified to be running a parish. And now he was already publicising the fact to the first parishioner he meets. What was he thinking?

However, this particular parishioner appeared to remain entirely unaffected by his revelation. Instead, she merely asked, in a somewhat detached fashion, 'Shall I give you a tour of the church? I can then talk you through the timetable for the weekend's services.'

Before Father Luca was able to follow the figure receding briskly into the main church, his phone rang. 'I'm so sorry. Could I just take this?' he called after Katie, who came to an impatient halt at the back of the church.

'Ciao papa, come va?' It was his dad. Father Luca understood that his parents were really alarmed at the situation he had found himself embroiled in, and needed all the reassurance he could give them. He was doing his best. Yes, he was eating well. Yes, he was sleeping okay. No, he wasn't about to be arrested for conspiracy to murder. At least one of these was true. For now.

Father Luca knew that asking after their family dog was probably a good way to steer the conversation away from the topic of stabbed parish priests. Their beloved Labrador was a subject that his father would relish talking about. The tactic seemed to work. For the moment anyway.

Once satisfied that his parents felt their son would live to see another day, he returned his attentions to the matter in hand.

Katie stood restlessly waiting for him.

'Sorry about that,' apologised Father Luca.

46

'No problem,' she replied somewhat curtly. 'We'll have a look around the main church, and then we are allowed to pop into Father Joseph's house to have a look at his diary. We can work out what you are able to cover and what we will need to postpone for now. Obviously, we can't get into the sacristy today, but you will have to get some sort of access on Sunday.' With that, she turned and walked briskly up one side of the church.

Father Luca was bewildered. He could understand the sorrow and grief of someone who had probably known Father Joseph all her life; he could grasp the reluctance to accept the change in circumstances. Yet in those first few minutes, this girl, now with her back turned coldly to him, had shown a warmth and curiosity that he had been obliged to politely ignore with practised ease.

Father Luca had chosen this path specifically to avoid the perils that accompanied the workings of the human heart. He no longer courted attention; he had ceased to reciprocate even when it was forthcoming. He donned his clerical garments as he would armour. They were a means of protection, not denial. For the past two years, his indifference had defined him.

Yet Father Luca, perhaps more accustomed to unrequited female admiration than he liked to admit, was unsettled by Katie's change of stance. He was rather keen to make amends for whatever offence he had committed. What on earth had he said to put her off him like this?

'I'm so sorry about Father Joseph,' he said solemnly as he caught up with Katie. 'How long had you known him?'

At this, Katie looked over her shoulder at Father Luca, frowning, 'Two years. But I've already told the police everything I know.'

'Of course. Sorry, I wasn't intending to interrogate you,' assured Father Luca, now distinctly on edge.

The tour of the church continued in an uncomfortable silence. Father Luca could only assume that this girl had an intense dislike of Italy for some mysterious reason.

It was only when the pair of them were outside, heading towards the presbytery, the house that had been home to Father Joseph, that Katie broke into a smile. A lively cocker spaniel bounded towards them, jumping up at Katie. Rubbing its head playfully, she laughed off the owner's apologies, and watched, grinning, as he gently pulled the dog on its way.

As they continued towards the front door, Katie asked, almost congenially, 'How old is your dog?' pulling out a large bunch of keys.

'Seven, nearly eight,' replied Father Luca with slight relief. And some confusion. He was finding it hard to keep up, to be honest.

Who knows? Maybe she sensed his vulnerability. Katie appeared as young as he was. Surely, she could understand the enormity of this task for someone like him?

'Come on in,' she said, more or less affably. 'I've got some milk on me. I know where the teabags are. Let's have a cup of tea while we try and make head or tail of what you will need to do.'

It was while Katie was making the tea that it occurred to Father Luca that this girl, with her apparent dislike of Italy, seemed to understand the language pretty well.

The phone conversation with his father had been entirely in Italian.

Chapter Thirteen

The assembled detectives waited restlessly as Detective Sergeant Thorne attempted to position a desk fan where it might provide a little relief in the uncomfortably warm meeting room. Jackets had been removed, shirt sleeves rolled up, everyone caught out by the rise in temperature.

DI Sloane sipped on his cup of water as he stood up to address his colleagues.

'Right, having spoken to a number of you, I just want to fill everyone in on what we have come up with so far on the Father Joseph case. Forensics have confirmed that the cause of death was a single stab wound to the abdomen. There were no signs of blunt force trauma, apart from a slight abrasion on the back of his head. This would have been most likely caused by a fall, following the stabbing. There were no defence wounds, no signs of a struggle, and no signs of any forced entry. This would suggest that either the killer was known to the victim or completely took him by surprise. Or both.

Although it was difficult for the Forensics team to judge, there didn't appear to be anything of significance or value missing from the sacristy or from the priest's house. Apart from Father Joseph's mobile phone, which has not been located as yet. So, it's looking as though burglary was not the motive.

In all likelihood, the mobile phone was taken by someone possibly wanting to cover their tracks. Someone who was known to the victim and had been in communication with him. Unfortunately, the last trace on

49

the phone was at the crime scene. Whoever did this had the foresight to switch it off before they took it anywhere.

Family Liaison Officers have managed to speak to quite a few altar boys and girls and their families. The team found a list of contacts at the house. That was an angle we needed to follow up immediately, of course. But to be honest, no one's got a bad word to say about him.

Which makes this whole situation all the more unfathomable. Father Joseph Boletti appears to have been a much-loved figure in this community.

Some of you, I know, have managed to speak to those in attendance at the Mass on that Wednesday morning. They were pretty much all long-standing members of St Anthony's church, and, by all accounts, spoke very fondly of their parish priest. Due to the general demographic, it would appear that most of them would struggle to throw their hymn books at the victim, never mind plunge a blade into him.

There were a number of fingerprints found in the sacristy, all of which we have matched with prints taken from the altar servers and Maria Fernandez. There were no fingerprints whatsoever on the envelope opener, the weapon used in this murder. And no attempt was made to remove the blade from the crime scene. This would suggest the assailant was wearing gloves at the time. I don't know many people who would just happen to have gloves on them in June. So, was this murder premeditated?

The graffiti on the wall would certainly add to that argument. Forensics have carried out some preliminary analysis of the paint. Unfortunately, it appears to be a widely available spray paint, but it might be worth asking around local DIY stores with regard to recent purchases.'

Sloane pointed to the photograph of the large eye that had been scrawled roughly on the wall of the sacristy. 'Does this image hold the key to the motive here? Was this line running down from the eye surplus to the design or was it meant to be a tear, suggesting sorrow? What message did the killer intend to leave? And why?'

Thorne raised his arm tentatively, an unsightly sweat patch visible under his arm. 'Sir, what if it was the evil eye?' he suggested, flicking hurriedly through his notepad with the other hand. Unable to locate the desired information, he continued uneasily, 'I think that eye was something to do with protection from evil rather than being actually evil in itself.'

Sloane viewed Thorne through narrowed eyes as the young sergeant returned to his search, head bowed low over his notes.

'Anything else from anyone?' he asked, looking around the room, a frown still etched on his forehead.

'I know there's a couple of you working on the victim's early years in Italy. We know now that Father Joseph grew up as Giuseppe Boletti in a place called Ravenna in north-east Italy. It's a town known more for its mosaics than any sort of criminal activity. All sounds pretty innocuous really. He went on to train to be a priest in Assisi, where Luca Rossetti is now studying. So there seems to be a completely plausible connection there.

But why did Father Joseph end up over here in England? First in Kent, and then in Haddelton? Why did he come here all those years ago? Keep delving there. See what you can come up with.'

Sloane turned to the whiteboard behind him, pointing vaguely towards the names taken from the flower-arranging rota. 'We have managed to speak to one of these ladies so far. Katie Evans. A pleasant enough young woman. She seemed as shocked and bewildered as everybody else we've spoken to. But she didn't really have any answers as to why someone would murder her parish priest.'

'Something that's a bit of a long shot, but could be interesting, Sir,' offered a young female detective from the back of the room. 'Parking restrictions around St Anthony's church make it very hard for anyone without a residents' permit to leave their vehicle parked in the vicinity for any length of time.

We've identified someone who received a parking fine twice in the last month, both times on a Saturday morning, one week apart. Both times they were in Briar Avenue, both times between 10am and 11am.'

'Okay,' replied Sloane noncommittally. 'But how would that be relevant to a murder committed on a Wednesday?'

'Well, the thing is, Sir, we did a couple of background checks. This man is on the system. A couple of minor offences as a teenager. He is originally from around here, but his current address is out in Woking, so a good forty-minute drive from here.'

'Great work. But what happens on a Saturday morning that would make him drive all the way over here for ten o'clock two weeks in a row, incurring parking fines while he is at it?' A note of intrigue had entered Sloane's voice.

'Well, I did a bit of checking, and there was something, Sir.' The young policewoman appeared to be getting quite excited.

'Confessions at St Anthony's run between ten o'clock and eleven o'clock on Saturday mornings.' She couldn't seem to get her words out quickly enough now.

'Confessions? Right. I want him in for questioning. Tomorrow. What's this man's name?'

'It's a Mr Nigel Ward. Aged thirty-eight. Based in Woking, as I said. Works as an accountant. I'll try and get hold of him after this.'

DS Thorne, who by now had located the relevant notes, was still keen to share his findings. Although perhaps the moment had passed. 'So,' he read carefully, 'In ancient Egyptian religion, the Eye of Horus represented protection, healing and restoration. It actually fits in with the whole Confession business, doesn't it? I think I'm going to have a bit of a trawl through the church records to see if this man has any history with St Anthony's church.'

Looking up, he was unable to decipher the expression on Sloane's face.

'If that's okay with you, Sir?'

'Worth a try, I suppose,' conceded Sloane evenly, as he motioned that the meeting had drawn to a close.

'While you're doing that, I need to pay another visit to Maria Fernandez,' he added. 'Interestingly, a large amount of fresh furniture polish was found wiped across the table next to the victim. I mean, how much polishing can you actually do before you notice a dead body lying on the floor next to you? Or was the polishing done afterwards, I wonder?'

Chapter Fourteen

Father Luca glanced around the sizeable, cluttered study that served somewhat inadequately as the parish office. Folders, bulging, disorderly, dusty, lined the countless shelves. The heavy antique desk was barely visible, obscured by casually discarded documents vying for space with religious artefacts, some surprisingly idiosyncratic. A snow globe housing the Virgin Mary jostled with a cartoon Pope Francis coffee mug, in turn housing a selection of brightly coloured book marks and pens bearing the names of popular places of pilgrimage.

Father Luca had had some limited experience of the impact of bereavement during his training in Assisi so far, and he recognised now that overwhelming sense of poignancy that arises at the sight of the redundant possessions of the person lost. The items rendered superfluous before the reality of their death has even hit you. Mundane objects transformed into treasures, the innocuous now assuming an unimaginably precious nature.

A sudden shriek startled Father Luca out of his melancholy contemplations. In one corner of the study, at a narrow unit equipped with a sink, an electric kettle and an assortment of mugs, Katie was preparing their cups of tea. She had one hand positioned under cold running water and was mopping up spilt water from the kettle with the other.

'Everything okay over there?' he asked, slightly alarmed.

'Yes, all good. Apart from scalding my hand with boiling water,' she laughed, grimacing. 'But I think I'll survive. Do you want milk or sugar?'

'Just milk please. Goodness, I hope your hand is alright.'

Father Luca watched as Katie removed the teabags, pressing them first near the rim of their mugs, and then poured in the milk in stages, stirring all the while in order to establish that the correct shade of tea had been achieved. It was a ritual as British as they come. Yet, despite his English heritage, it was not something that he adhered to back home in Italy. There, coffee reigned supreme, milky and frothy in the morning, short and sweet after lunch. Coffee was something that Father Luca would not be giving up for Lent any time soon.

But right now, in the gloom of this dingy study, away from the glare of the sun that blazed outside, as he took the chipped mug that Katie proffered, this felt bizarrely like coming home. He was curious to know more about this enigmatic English girl. Who didn't like Italy. Or priests maybe? Especially Italian priests.

He decided to chance it.

'So, what's your connection with St Anthony's?' he asked as casually as he could.

A moment's hesitation from Katie had him fearing the worst. But as he glanced over towards her, kicking himself, he saw she was smiling. Sort of. Well, she wasn't glaring at him.

'It was through the school really. My son goes to the local Catholic primary school.'

'Oh, you have a son?'

'Yes. Alex is nearly six. It's just him and me. I mean, I don't have any other children. It's just the two of us,' Katie laughed awkwardly. Father Luca gathered from this that there was no Mr Evans around. Why on earth did he feel rather pleased? The poor girl was potentially a struggling, single mother, dealing with the fall-out of a failed marriage, or maybe coping with a recent bereavement. He was surprised at himself.

'It's very good of you to help out at St Anthony's. Life must be very busy with a five-year-old. Though I can imagine an extra pair of hands must have been very welcome here. It all looks a bit chaotic, judging by this room.'

'I had only really just started getting involved. The person who had been doing it for years retired and moved away a few months back. I think Father Joseph was desperate, and I just couldn't say no. I work part-time as a freelance translator, fitting my hours around Alex, so I didn't really have an excuse.'

'Translator? What a great job. Which languages do you translate into? Or from?'

Katie paused before her reply came, 'Italian actually.'

'*Allora parliamo in italiano,*' joked Father Luca. 'Wow, that's a coincidence. Did you study it at university?'

'Not exactly,' she replied vaguely.

Father Luca's smiled faded abruptly as he caught Katie's eye. She was suddenly looking at him with such deep suspicion and uncertainty.

'Why all the questions?' she demanded. 'Why are you really here?'

Father Luca placed his mug slowly on the desk. 'Look, the police have questioned me and have spoken with the relevant authorities back in Italy. I can assure you I had absolutely nothing to do with the death of Father Joseph. I am as upset and shocked as you are.'

The eyes that had been staring at his so searchingly suddenly filled and brimmed over.

'I'm not talking about the threat to poor Father Joseph's safety. I'm talking about the threat to my own safety. And Alex's.'

Chapter Fifteen

Detective Inspector Sloane was back in Maria Fernandez's living room. With Thorne opting to do a little digging into church records, it was a young police officer in uniform who sat next to him. Both had been granted the comfort of a position on the sofa today, with Doreen apparently busy elsewhere. Maria sat on the armchair opposite them, composed, expectant.

'Miss Fernandez,' began Sloane, clearing his throat, 'Some new information has come to light that we need to ask you a couple of questions about.'

Maria's eyes widened and her chest rose. 'Of course, Inspector. I will do whatever it takes to bring to justice the monster that carried out this vile act.'

'We just need to go over a few details that we may have possibly covered before. Just for clarity,' explained Sloane, as he wondered to himself why he was nervously attempting to soften the blow here.

'Our colleagues in Forensics discovered a significant amount of fresh furniture polish on the table in the sacristy, but none in the main church. Would you be able to provide any explanation for this? I understand that you had been about to start some cleaning.'

There was a brief silence, and those smouldering, brown eyes blinked a couple of times.

'I think it was the shock, the horror of what I could see. I think I must have just pressed down on the can of polish without realising, a sort of automatic response.'

'Miss Fernandez, the furniture polish had been wiped in with a duster. Forensics found a number of fibres. Are you going to tell me that you automatically rubbed away at that table while you stood aghast over the body of your parish priest?'

Another silence ensued. Chin raised, lips pursed, nostrils flared, Maria Fernandez tossed her hair back defiantly.

'Oh, for goodness' sake, are you accusing me of murdering Father Joseph?'

'Well, did you?' asked Sloane, somewhat boldly, he felt.

'Of course I didn't kill him!'

Maria's eyes blazed as she fixed them on the startled detective.

'I loved him!'

And with that, she began to wail inconsolably.

Chapter Sixteen

Detective Sergeant Thorne tapped impatiently on the door of St Anthony's presbytery, Father Joseph's home until earlier this week. He was rather perturbed that some fine detective work on his part threatened to be obstructed by the presence of two of the witnesses in this very enquiry. Pretty unbelievable really, he thought. What was Sloane thinking giving them all this access to the property?

To be honest, Thorne couldn't really understand why they were both still there. Had they really needed two hours to check the times of the Sunday services? He couldn't comprehend, either, why the young Italian priest opened the door so nervously, suspicion written all over his face. Or actually, maybe he could. After what had happened to the last priest in charge here. Rather him than me, he thought.

'Oh, Inspector, it's you,' he said with some relief.

DS Thorne did not correct him, delighted at his promotion.

'Actually, we were just leaving,' Father Luca continued. 'We need to get some lunch. Do you want to keep hold of the keys for now? I'm sure your need is greater than ours.'

From behind him, a tear-stained face appeared at the doorway. 'Hello again,' said Katie, passing the bunch of keys to Thorne. Her visible distress only strengthened his conviction that the key to this crime lay in the past. No one had said a negative word about this priest; this was clearly a community in shock, bereft. Father Joseph Boletti was being described as charming, charismatic, kind and funny by everyone who knew him. Why on earth was he brutally murdered this week?

The young sergeant knew they had a significant challenge on their hands with this case. There were so many unanswered questions. Had this benevolent soul come into possession of information that had led to his death? Or had Father Joseph's murder really been an act of revenge? But what for? And was there a connection with Italy somehow?

In the meantime, DS Thorne was certainly right about the affection felt for Father Joseph, but his interpretation of the tears on Katie Evans' face could not have been more wrong.

Chapter Seventeen

In Maria Fernandez's living-room, DI Sloane and the young police officer glanced briefly at one another. Sloane inclined his head towards the box of tissues, and the young policeman levered himself up awkwardly from the depths of Maria's cushions to pass her the much-needed hankies.

Maria wiped delicately at the tears that streamed down her face.

Sloane cleared his throat. 'Miss Fernandez, this is clearly all very distressing for you, and I am sorry to have to push you on this. But could you explain exactly what you meant just now when you said that you, er, loved Father Joseph?'

Maria sighed theatrically. 'Don't apologise,' she replied. 'Actually, this is a relief...after all these years. You can't imagine what it has been like for me, and what it is like now. I loved him with all my heart and have done so for twenty years. For twenty years, I stayed quietly by his side, in the shadows. He just couldn't bring himself to make a choice. You know, whenever I see that Princess Diana interview, I know exactly how she felt. There were three of us in the relationship; Joseph, myself, and...'

Maria flung her arms upwards, pointing towards upstairs. Sloane and the young officer, already astounded by Maria's startling revelation, craned their necks backwards, eyes on the ceiling, both wondering who else could possibly have been involved in this *ménage à trois*.

Fortunately, Maria was still in full flow, and barely noticed the officers' confusion.

'God. His duty to God.' The sobbing started anew.

'Right,' ventured Sloane. 'We will obviously need to discuss the nature of your relationship with Father Joseph in a little more detail at some point. Clearly, you were closer to him than other parishioners. But for now, can I ask you if there was anything at all that Father Joseph had said or done that had given you cause for concern? Anything that might have had a connection with his death?'

Maria met Sloane's eye with a look of utter despair. 'Actually, there was. About two weeks ago, he confided in me that he might have to leave St Anthony's, possibly for good. That was why he was arranging for the young priest to be around. Just in case.'

'Just in case of what?'

'That's just it. I have no idea.'

'Miss Fernandez, how did you feel about the idea of Father Joseph leaving?'

'I was devastated. I had built my whole life around him. We met in Santiago de Compostela twenty years ago where we were both on pilgrimages. I was already in my thirties by then. I had been unlucky in love, I suppose. I hadn't found my Mr Right. And then I was introduced to Joseph. I knew he was out of bounds, this handsome, funny, Italian priest. I knew it was wrong. But for me, it was love at first sight, I just couldn't help myself. It was as though I had been struck by lightning - but in a good way, of course. We stayed in touch, and I left my home country two years later to be close to him. I hope I am not betraying his trust now when I tell you that my love was reciprocated.'

Maria dabbed at her eyes delicately.

'Our love affair was destined to remain a secret. He was so strict about it all. Please, please do not think badly of Joseph. He was a good man. He served his parish loyally. His only crime was to fall in love.'

Maria's sobs could still be heard as Sloane pulled her front door closed behind him. He realised too late that he had failed to establish any credible reason for all the dusting and polishing that had taken place on the day of the murder. Compounding this, Maria Fernandez had admitted that her great love was planning to walk out of her life. Could this woman, clearly of a tempestuous nature, be capable of a crime of passion, he wondered, knocking gently on the neighbouring door? Doreen's distressed neighbour may yet be deemed guilty of murder, but for now she was in need of tea and sympathy, and a bearer of tissues.

Chapter Eighteen

DS Thorne surveyed with a sinking heart the seemingly infinite number of shelves in Father Joseph's study, several of them bowing under the weight of the folders and documents piled upon them. His enthusiasm only returned when, on closer inspection, he spotted dates scrawled in thick felt-tip along the spines of most of the files. His intention had been to focus initially on documents dating back thirty-eight years, when Nigel Ward had been born. If he had been christened there, that would at least establish a link with this church.

Having brushed away at the dust that coated the older files, Thorne pulled out a bulging mass of documentation, thinly encased in flimsy cardboard, dated simply 1985.

The precarious nature of this package necessitated a swift transfer to the nearby desk, nudging both the receiver of the little-used landline phone and the snow globe next to it, setting the tiny, joyful snowflakes incongruously in motion. It soon became clear, as Thorne began turning the brittle, faded pages, that each and every parish occurrence that year was contained in this folder. It was full of all manner of certificates, newspaper cuttings and photographs.

He was just starting to regret his decision to single-handedly solve this case, when he came across a torn-out diary page for the month of March, detailing a wedding day, a couple of funerals, and a christening. The name of the baby being christened was Nigel Ward, the man who had returned to St Anthony's all these years later, clearly with the need to unburden his soul. Twice.

What had he done? What had he revealed to Father Joseph? And had it resulted in the priest's murder?

Elated at his discovery, Thorne took a photograph of the page with his phone, and then continued to flick hurriedly through the pieces of paper, not entirely sure if there was any longer a point to this exercise. He stopped at a large colour photograph of a procession of children; the girls in white dresses with veils, all satin and lace, their hands clasped in prayer, rosary beads dangling from their wrists; the boys in their smartest jackets, a bright red sash looping down from one shoulder. Solemnity and smiles all round.

Thorne was not particularly familiar with the Catholic religion; it all felt a little foreign to him if he was honest. It was only by turning the photograph over that he discovered this was a First Holy Communion Mass. It was dated May 1985, so of no particular relevance to his research into Nigel Ward, who would only have been a few months old at the time.

Yet, as he was about to slide the glossy piece of paper back into position, his eye caught the priest presiding over events from the altar in the background. His image was blurred, unlit. But it was almost certainly the elderly priest who had accompanied the young Italian over to St Anthony's this morning. It wasn't necessary for Thorne to rustle through too many pages of the surrounding documentation to discover that Father O'Leary was indeed the parish priest at this time.

As he stared more intently at the photograph, he noticed the figure leading the procession down the aisle, eyes cast upward towards the long, narrow, gold cross that he held aloft, far older and taller than the children behind him, white robes billowing as he guided them out of St Anthony's. Thorne's brow furrowed in disbelief as recognition dawned.

66

The teenager was none other than Robert Sloane, the Detective Inspector leading the investigation into a murder at the very same church.

Chapter Nineteen

No sooner had they sat down than Katie's mobile phone started to buzz.

'Sorry,' she said apologetically, 'I'd better check my messages, just in case it's the school about Alex.'

'Absolutely,' replied Father Luca. 'I'll have a quick look through the menu. Hope everything's okay.'

They were tucked in the corner of a nearby pub overlooking the river Thames currently glinting in the sunlight. The place was almost deserted inside on this glorious day, most customers preferring to take advantage of the cramped outside space, with its parasols unfurled and a riot of colour trailing from its many pots.

Indoors, the pub's dark panelled walls, punctuated occasionally with framed images of life on the river, and coupled with the heavy wooden furniture they now occupied, afforded this couple the privacy they sought.

Lunch with a young female parishioner was not something that Father Luca had foreseen happening on the first day of his foray into ministerial duties here in Haddelton. However, the murder of his prospective host had been rather unexpected too, he guessed. And the last two hours, spent in the company of Katie Evans, were proving that circumstances were not about to get any less complicated or worrying.

A snort of laughter distracted Father Luca from his deliberations over the offerings on the menu. Like every self-respecting Italian, he would always favour his own country's cuisine, really only trying alternatives out of a sense of politeness or a lack of options. He had to admit he had noticed a considerable improvement in the Italian food served in England in recent years, brought over, of course, by his fellow countrymen. It was definitely less generic now, he conceded, less afraid of the simplicity that lay at the heart of so many of his country's dishes. But for now, it was going to be breaded cod or a chicken burger.

'Oh, that's so funny,' laughed Katie, still reading the phone in her hand. 'Both my friends who were supposed to be speaking to the police later have been told that their meetings have been postponed 'due to ongoing developments in the enquiry'. They are both furious. I'm not sure if they've actually got anything relevant to say, but they were definitely looking forward to all the drama of it.'

'I'm sure they'll get their turn. Probably next week now,' Luca replied. 'I wonder what these developments are? I do hope they get to the bottom of all this as soon as possible. What if there is a serial killer on the prowl who has murderous intent when it comes to Catholic priests in the local area? I could be the very next target.'

Katie raised her eyes to look across at the charming, gentle soul sitting opposite her; so genuine, so approachable, so easy to confide in. Just like Father Joseph, the only other person she had dared to share her past with. Killed earlier this week.

And now this young priest carried her secrets too.

Chapter Twenty

SATURDAY

Nigel Ward's aftershave still lingered in the interview room, even as his sleek, expensive car reached the motorway that would take him back home to Woking. DS Thorne eyed DI Sloane with uncertainty.

'Thoughts?' asked Sloane, sipping his tea, oblivious to the turmoil in his sergeant's head.

The Inspector was still nursing some doubts of his own, of course. What had happened to that mobile phone? Who had taken it? And how could he get it back?

'I definitely think he is holding something back,' replied Thorne truthfully.

'You're not wrong there,' agreed Sloane. 'His whole story just felt a little rehearsed.'

'At least he admitted that he did go to Father Joseph for Confession.'

'Yes, only after you'd implied that he'd been captured on CCTV walking towards the church. Don't do that again. For God's sake, there isn't a camera anywhere close.'

'Well, he knew the parking fines had given him away already,' Thorne smirked. 'I just don't buy the idea that he would travel all this way, two weeks in a row, to go to Confession in a church he hadn't set foot in for nearly thirty years; that he's a bit of a born-again Christian these days and got nostalgic about St Anthony's.'

'Yes, it's strange,' agreed Sloane. 'By his own admission, he was a reluctant adherent of the religion he was born into. Why the sudden change of heart? Something just doesn't add up.'

'Well, he definitely had things to confess. He was a bit of a tearaway for a while. Charges for being drunk and disorderly, speeding and affray. All by his early twenties.'

'Seems to have turned his life around though. Nice house, wife, children, successful career as an accountant. And was apparently hard at work in his office, surrounded by colleagues, all day Wednesday. He's got at least half a dozen people happy to confirm his whereabouts at the time of the murder.' Sloane was checking back through his notes.

Thorne turned to watch him. 'It's odd in a way that he came back to the church he knew, but not the priest. Do you really believe he had no connection to Father Joseph, as he wasn't setting foot in St Anthony's by the time he came along?' He paused. 'It's Father O'Leary that he remembers.'

As Sloane guardedly looked up, the expression on Thorne's face told the Inspector that the inevitable had happened. Thorne had blurred the lines; got too close.

To Thorne's astonishment, DI Sloane placed his head in his hands and started to sob quietly.

Chapter Twenty-One

The enormous canopies of the trees in Bushy Park, oaks, limes, silver maples and black poplars, all bore their dense foliage majestically, denying the late morning sunlight passage to the ground beneath them. The deer, free to roam, appeared to seek the shade they offered, clustering around them to idly chew. The seemingly infinite expanse of grass, nourished by the recent inclement weather, shone emerald green, reflecting the sun's rays; the sky above was a sheet of vivid blue, the occasional uniform strip of vapour trail migrating across it, a pinpoint of a plane at its head, silent and unnoticed.

Birdsong, conversation and laughter had erupted all around, marking the arrival of a long-anticipated summer. The main pathways were busy. Red-faced joggers panted loudly; cyclists swerved around those strolling, unaccustomed to the shorts and summer dresses they now wore, feeling self-conscious and exposed without their jackets and coats; dog-walkers smiled at the young parents pushing prams, toddlers in sun hats at their sides, arms smeared with suncream.

Katie smiled as she spotted Maggie. Dressed immaculately in a vibrant, strappy sun dress and gorgeously unsuitable sandals, her glamorous friend pulled her large sunglasses up onto her head and waved. Alex, having already noticed her and Noah, was almost with them, his scooter giving him a considerable advantage over Katie, weighed down with their picnic bag.

'So, it's just us then in the end?' asked Katie as she reached the picnic blanket, where two large plastic wine glasses were the only items that had been removed so far from Maggie's wicker hamper.

'Yes, Elizabeth had to go and collect Olivia from university in the end. She needed to get all her stuff back for the summer. I think she's moving into a different student house next year. I said I'd look after Tom for the day and he could just play with our two for the afternoon. But he really wanted to go up to Birmingham with Elizabeth.'

'Fair enough. Goodness, that'll be us before we know it,' said Katie, setting down her bag to retrieve her picnic rug.

'Tell me about it. I've just started Oliver with a new tutor. That's where he is now. Philip will pick him up if he can drag himself away from the cricket.'

'Tutoring? On a Saturday? That's just cruel,' laughed Katie.

'It's not forever, but I had to get in quick as she's meant to be so good. He'll be sitting all those dreaded entrance exams next year, and he's got to know his stuff. No pressure!' she laughed as she passed one of her wine glasses to Katie.

'Now, I hope you don't think it inappropriate, what with everything that has happened this week, but I do think we both need a large glass of wine, don't you?'

Her question was clearly purely rhetorical, for, as she spoke, a generous amount of chilled white wine was being poured determinedly into Katie's glass.

'So,' Maggie continued, as Katie settled into a position where she could keep an eye on Alex and Noah, now clambering on a nearby log. 'I want to know everything. What did the police ask you? Why are we no longer in the frame at the moment? Who do they think did it?'

'To be honest, I don't think we were ever their prime suspects. I think they were really looking for any background information they could get from us. I actually can't even remember what I said now. I was so nervous. Really scared I was going to say something that would incriminate me.' Katie took a large gulp of her wine. 'Anyway, don't worry, I'm sure you'll get your turn eventually.'

Maggie lowered her voice, glancing around, 'Between you and me, I am worried, Katie.'

'About what? You'll be absolutely fine.'

'I can't stop thinking about what has happened. And why it has happened. And who would want to do it. I've even been formulating a few theories of my own. The more I think about it, the more everyone is a suspect,' Maggie whispered. 'I just don't know whether I will end up voicing my suspicions under the pressure of an interrogation. I don't want to send the detectives on a wild goose chase, but obviously if I have information that could help solve this crime, I feel it is my duty to pass it on.'

'Firstly, it will not be an interrogation, Maggie. It is quite nerve-wracking, but they will literally just ask you where you were that morning, and how well you knew Father Joseph, that sort of thing. Secondly, I hope you are not going to mention me when you launch into your list of suspects.'

'No, not you, don't worry. Even though you are a bit of a dark horse at times,' smiled Maggie.

She then paused, 'If I tell you something, will you promise not to say anything to anyone? I feel really bad even thinking it, but it keeps going round and round in my head, and I need a second opinion on the whole thing.'

'Go ahead, Miss Marple, I'm intrigued. My lips are sealed.'

'Well, don't you think it's strange that Elizabeth has never confided in us who Olivia's father is? I know we've only known her since the boys started in Reception, but it's nearly two years now, and we are definitely closer to her than any of the other parents at the school. And before you say it, I know that she's really happy with Greg now, and maybe it's just that the subject has become taboo.' Maggie took a deep breath and frowned.

Katie looked at her quizzically. 'I don't get where you're going with this. Are you suggesting that after a brief teenage encounter nearly twenty years ago, resulting in the unforeseen arrival of a gorgeous baby girl, the other party involved has returned to wreak revenge for his denied paternal rights, starting with Elizabeth's parish priest? It all sounds very tenuous to be honest.' She was laughing now.

But her mirth was not reciprocated

'Just think about it, Katie. Elizabeth is a blue-eyed blonde, as is Tom, with his dad, Greg, being pretty fair himself. But look at Olivia. Her jet-black hair, dark brown eyes, her olive skin. Elizabeth was barely sixteen when she gave birth to Olivia, and her life was put on hold. She had years on her own bringing up that baby, relying on hand-outs from friends and family. It was a miserable existence. Until she met Greg, she really struggled.'

Maggie took a large gulp of wine, but her eyes did not leave Katie's.

'Now, at fifteen, you don't tend to go that far afield generally. Although the inclination may be there, life hasn't really taken off at that age, has it? So, who would Elizabeth have come into contact with, possibly on a regular basis? Who would her probably very religious family have trusted unquestioningly?'

'Oh my God, you don't think Father Joseph was Olivia's father? Wouldn't he have been a bit old for her?'

'Well, a bit yes. He would have been in his late thirties. But I can imagine he was a very attractive man. Classically tall, dark and handsome. And I bet Elizabeth was just blossoming at that age – fresh for the picking, hey?'

Katie shook her head. She felt a bit sick. 'No, I just can't see it. I don't want to believe it of either of them. And anyway, even if this were all true, how would it be connected to Father Joseph's murder?'

'Well, what if they had an argument? What if things escalated? All that resentment building up over the years, all the hardship she suffered, her anger finally spilling over as she accosted him in that secluded room. Don't forget, none of us were together that morning. We only have each other's word as to where we were. None of us have a concrete alibi.'

The colour drained from Katie's face. 'Maggie, what are you saying?'

'I think Elizabeth might have killed Father Joseph.'

Chapter Twenty-Two

Father Luca lay in the narrow single bed in Father O'Leary's box room, eyes wide open, staring up at the Artex ceiling. Every so often, a night bus would sail past the small window to his side, lighting up the dark, austerely furnished room. In recent times, he had become more accustomed to the ascetic lifestyle of a seminarian; he had willingly embraced a humble, modest, unadorned existence.

Yet, if the truth be told, all that simplicity and restraint was far easier to cope with in the delightful surroundings of Assisi, where beauty assailed you at every turn. Self-denial was effectively an impossibility as your senses soaked up the sights, the smells, the tastes and the sounds of that beautiful town. The feeling of warmth of the sun on your skin; the aromas emanating from the wonderful restaurants dotted along the narrow, cobbled streets; the vibrant colours of the sunlit architecture. He had to admit, it all certainly helped to offset any abstinence or lack of self-indulgence.

All this self-sacrifice suddenly felt a whole lot more noticeable in Father O'Leary's box room. He gazed up at the bare lightbulb hanging from the ceiling and sighed.

Sleep would not come to Father Luca. Yet it was neither the buses, nor the small, rigid bed, that kept him awake. Naturally, he was experiencing a degree of nervousness at the prospect of saying Mass the following day, leading a parish in mourning, a community in shock. But for that, for the most part, he knew the script. Following the advice from Father O'Leary, Father Luca was keeping the sermon as brief as possible. It would be a few carefully chosen words that would acknowledge the bereavement and offer some comfort.

With officers in attendance, he had been able to access the sacristy that afternoon to retrieve all that would be needed in the morning. That moment in itself had been shocking enough to deny Father Luca the sleep that eluded him. He had been unable to prevent himself from looking down at where he imagined the body would have lain, blood stains, distressingly, confirming his suspicions. The graffiti on the wall had been unexpected, startling him. He had been warned not to discuss anything he noticed within the room so as not to jeopardise the enquiry, and had made sure not to comment to the police officers, who had merely observed him neutrally in silence.

It was really hard to comprehend that the jovial soul, who had so recently been urging him to throw caution to the wind and join him here, had met such a grisly fate at this very spot. Could there have been a connection between his sudden request and the murder that had ensued? Had Father Joseph been aware that his life was in danger?

Yet, despite the horror of that room today, and notwithstanding his nerves about the following day, something else was preventing slumber for the young priest lying awake so late into the night.

Katie.

Her story, spilling out so suddenly yesterday, had taken him by surprise. And the fact that she had chosen to confide in him. He understood by now that priests, like doctors, exempt from the social norms, became bearers of confidences, all manner of private worries delivered at their feet with an expectation of discretion and professional wisdom.

But what advice had he really been able to give her though? What help could he be to this young woman who had resorted to such desperate measures? Who now lived in fear of discovery? Taking flight under cover of night, disappearing without trace. This was not behaviour he could usually condone. She had torn a child away from much of its family, the boy's memories barely formed, too vague to stand the test of time.

He was now, of course, complicit in her deception, an unwitting accomplice. He knew he would need to act.

And yet. Did her actions warrant exposure? It was not cruelty or malice that had prompted her decision to do what she did. It was desperation.

To discover that Katie had actually been living in Italy, of all places, had been pretty incredible. But Father Luca's eyes had widened all the more as she had begun to divulge the details of her years spent in his home country; the carefree first year teaching English in Rome, fresh out of university and looking for adventure, bonding with new friends over exquisite pasta and the heavenly local wines, enjoying the delights of this glorious city and the attention of the handsome young men who lived there; meeting Leonardo during her second winter there. In his final year at university, due to return home to Puglia once he had gained his *laurea*, Leonardo had been so attentive and devoted. She had literally basked in his adulation. She couldn't have been happier.

Time passed, and Leonardo had eventually left Rome, but not before making Katie promise she would eventually join him in his home town of Taranto.

By now, Katie had created a wonderful life for herself in Rome. Her teaching job, her apartment, and her circle of friends all bore testament to the success of her move abroad.

She had been the only child of elderly parents. A belated but doted-upon arrival, her early childhood in Northumberland had been blissful, blighted only later by the sudden loss of her father, and the confusion and gradual, agonising loss of her mother in recent years. Her move to Italy had been a show of strength, a fearless gesture after all the pain and uncertainty.

Katie had created a family of sorts in Rome. Her colleagues, her students, her flatmates, she counted many of them as close personal friends. She had integrated into this proudly flamboyant, unapologetically glamorous world. And the thought of leaving it all behind had terrified her.

However, her deliberations were cut very short, and the decision was to be taken out of her hands rather rapidly. A weekend visit down to Puglia had resulted in a very public sweeping gesture from Leonardo. His mother, present along with several other family members, had cried even before Leonardo had produced the glittering ring, his beautiful face beseeching yet assured.

The wedding had taken place within a year, small by Italian standards, although the customary eight or nine courses and the obligation for guests to purchase excessively generous presents had remained. The absence of family on her side had been a source of pain, but she guessed it was one of the reasons she had found herself in this situation.

Katie was aware that Leonardo's family had initially had deep reservations when it came to his burgeoning romance with this unknown English girl. Yet as she slowly settled into married life with her new husband, she had seen only warmth and kindness in their eyes. Maybe it was all going to work out just fine, she'd thought.

Much to her relief, Katie had found work at an English Language School in the city centre, and she had relished the opportunity to revert to the language and humour of her home country, swapping anecdotes with colleagues while sipping cappuccinos near the Piazza Fontana before morning classes.

She would have joined them sometimes for an early evening *frizzantino* at the local bar to celebrate the end of the teaching day, but Leonardo had liked Katie to be at home with him in the evenings. With her mother-in-law's help, Katie was trying to extend her somewhat limited repertoire when it came to Italian cuisine. But Leonardo had never complained. He was simply content that his young wife was lovingly preparing the meals that were set upon his table every night.

When Katie had started to experience a nauseating hunger that had threatened to overwhelm her, she had drawn the only possible conclusion, and had taken stock. In all honesty, she had looked forward to the arrival of something that would be inherently hers, that she could take credit for. Her hope had been to retain some sort of control and independence when it came to the birth and upbringing of the child. In fairness, her parents-in-law had done their best to allow Katie some privacy initially, but instinct had prevailed, and for the duration of her miserable pregnancy, the prospective *nonni* had orchestrated their support with all the ardour and precision of a military operation.

Eventually, blue ribbons had adorned their front door, and an entire family had cooed and fretted in equal measure over the tiny new person in their lives.

For the new mother, elation had rapidly given way to exhaustion. Alessio had been a restless, fretful baby, and Katie was doing the lion's share of the childcare. During her pregnancy, while Katie had struggled with nausea and fatigue, Leonardo had taken up with some old acquaintances, lost during his years in Rome. Increasingly, during those first few months of Alessio's life, Leonardo had been inexplicably absent. Katie couldn't put her finger on it, but at times he had appeared somewhat indifferent, more lethargic, almost vacant. She had put it down to the strain of parenthood, and her focus had stayed trained, laser sharp, on her newly born son.

Katie hadn't noticed the fearful look in the eyes of Leonardo's parents; she hadn't heard the pleas addressed to their beloved son. It had been a considerable shock for her to open her front door and discover two thugs, all tattooed necks and angry eyes, demanding to speak to Leonardo. Her husband's arrival and the ensuing argument had revealed to Katie all she needed to know.

Leonardo's struggle with drugs had blighted the following two years of their marriage; optimism alternating with despair; rehabilitation interwoven with snarling rages and missing jewellery. She did all she could to protect Alessio from the erratic behaviour of his father, but the impact it was having on his young life was undeniable. Leonardo's parents had seemed blindly optimistic, passing off their son's increasingly alarming conduct as a phase, willing to forgive every broken promise, happy to comply with every plea for more cash.

Returning home one afternoon to find their apartment had been ransacked, Alessio's room turned upside down, had been the final straw for Katie.

She had swiftly gathered together a few items for herself and her son, grabbed the passports mercifully spared in the break-in, and taken a taxi to the airport in Bari, Alessio held tightly in her arms. The first available flight to the UK had been to Heathrow, paid for with savings from the bank account she had set up for herself in recent months, wisely concealed. The proceeds from the recent sale of her late parents' property in Northumberland had offered Katie a lifeline, a chance to start afresh. An opportunity to offer Alessio a safe, stable existence. As long as she remained anonymous, untraceable, all connections with Leonardo's family and Taranto broken.

She knew that Leonardo would search for her, distraught, humiliated, enraged at the disappearance of his wife and child. She was aware that these were desperate measures. But she had no choice. Leonardo now represented a possible threat to her son's life. And there was nothing she wouldn't do to protect him. This was all for Alessio.

Jumping into a taxi at Heathrow Airport with a tired, bewildered three-year-old that dark, drizzly evening, Katie had picked the brains of the driver in an effort to narrow down all the possible destinations that lay ahead. She didn't know London at all and had looked at him blankly as he had mentioned the various towns they would reach before too long. Twickenham she had heard of because of the rugby stadium, but she had never been there in her life; she'd certainly never heard of any of the surrounding towns; Haddelton didn't ring any bells whatsoever; she had absolutely no connection with the place; she wouldn't know where to start when it came to finding somewhere to stay; she wouldn't know a soul. It was perfect.

Father Luca turned onto his side and gazed out at the advertisement along the side of a passing bus. The words were just visible as the sky beyond began to lose its inky blackness, languidly paling, the streets below briefly grey and ordinary, until an orange glow gradually crept over the horizon, bathing everything in its warm radiance.

He sighed, not for the first time that night. Katie had been trapped in this self-inflicted, clandestine existence for two years now. Her years in Italy had been effectively erased. She had encouraged the belief that her move to Haddelton had been a fresh start after a failed marriage up in Northumberland. Alessio was now simply Alex.

On top of all this, Katie had literally dared to entrust one person with the truth. Father Joseph.

And now he was dead.

Father Luca would not find the comfort of dreams as dawn continued to break that morning.

Chapter Twenty-Three

SUNDAY

Katie surveyed her bedroom floor as she stood in front of her mirror. Nearly every item of clothing that she possessed lay in a heap, discarded with a groan of disapproval.

'Mummy, you look so pretty!' exclaimed Alex, padding into her room, catching sight of the floral dress his mother currently had on, all yellows and greens, set off by some little-worn jewellery that she had always considered a little bold. Her freshly-washed, auburn hair hung loose around her shoulders, caressing the freckles on her bare arms, her lips crimson.

'Oh, thank you, sweetie,' replied Katie, carefully rubbing off the red lipstick. Too much. Definitely too much, she decided. In fact, what on earth was she thinking? She knew Father Luca was out of bounds. And she was certainly not temptress material. Yes, she'd loved every minute of the day they'd spent together, but she already had one ill-fated relationship with an Italian behind her. Why, for heaven's sake, would she even be encouraging another? Heaven being the operative word here, of course. Not only was the intended recipient of all her efforts Italian, he was also on his way to becoming a priest. So, all in all, this was basically self-sabotage, wasn't it?

She pointedly removed all the jewellery from around her neck and wrists, and grabbed her bag. 'Right, Alex, off to church we go,' she said, ignoring the impulse to douse herself with her favourite perfume. Nevertheless, as Katie locked her front door behind them, she was still wearing that pretty summer dress.

Chapter Twenty-Four

Unsurprisingly, St Anthony's church was brimming with parishioners at half past ten that Sunday morning, the curious and the distraught sitting shoulder to shoulder in anticipation and shock. Katie, to her horror, noticed too late the blanket of sombre greys and blacks that filled the pews. Her almost luminous yellow dress suddenly felt utterly inappropriate. What had she been thinking? Here she was, the scarlet woman with a wiggle in her walk, her motives evident to all and sundry; indifferent to the solemnity of the occasion; instead, intent on fluttering her eyelashes at this handsome, young visitor.

Clutching Alex to her on one side, her bag positioned firmly on the other, Katie filed past her judge and jury, her kitten heels tapping embarrassingly loudly in the mournful silence. As she slotted into a couple of spaces next to Elizabeth, Katie found herself glancing furtively down at her friend's pale grey top. No giveaway blood spatters, she noted, hating herself for even entertaining the idea that her friend had thrust a blade into their parish priest. It was unthinkable. Absolutely out of the question.

Yet, Katie found that she couldn't quite look at her friend in the same way as they sat there waiting.

'Elizabeth, do you want to go for a coffee this week?' she whispered. 'I've been thinking about what could have happened to Father Joseph. I just wanted to pick your brain.'

Elizabeth hesitated.

'Well, I've got Pilates on Tuesday morning. Why don't I come over to yours afterwards as I'll be out and about already? The boys will be at school, so it'll just be the two of us.'

'Sounds good, thanks,' smiled Katie, as she began to look discreetly around for Maggie. Predictably, her elegant friend was managing to carry off a look that was suitably funereal but utterly chic. In her black, beautifully tailored shift dress, she stared solemnly ahead, the picture of grief. If the truth be told, it was academic aspiration, rather than religious devotion, that motivated Maggie to attend St Anthony's with such frequency. She was essentially covering all bases. The local Catholic secondary school was the perfect back-up if all the tutoring didn't pay off. The flower-arranging and cleaning at the church were, of course, all part of her master plan. It was all for the children really.

As the first hymn began, Katie turned her attention back to the altar, trying to ignore the butterflies in her stomach. She could only imagine how nervous Father Luca must be feeling right now. He had such huge boots to fill. But how lucky it was that he had arrived, and that he could take over for the next couple of months. Maybe three? She was more than happy to do anything to help out, help him settle in. She'd suddenly found someone to confide in, and he'd been so understanding and supportive. She just wanted to repay his kindness, that was all, she told herself. That was all it could ever be. He was just a young priest doing his best in the most difficult of circumstances.

A sudden wave of grief washed over her as it hit her yet again that Father Joseph had gone.

And while she sang, glancing from time to time towards Elizabeth, she couldn't help but wonder if his killer sat amongst them right now.

Chapter Twenty-Five

Father Luca stood outside St Anthony's church after the service, suffering from a severe case of imposter syndrome. He shook hands politely with the emerging parishioners, offering words of consolation, their faces more trusting, less suspicious than in those first few minutes of the Mass. The mood had been so sombre, so cheerless. He had seen the confusion and dismay in their eyes; he'd been all too aware of their grief and fear.

Katie alone had smiled comfortingly at him, a ray of sunlight breaking through a raft of dark cloud before him.

The news that a suitable replacement for Father Joseph had been found already, and would be arriving from Poland as soon as possible, had seemed to reassure this bleak congregation. He couldn't help but notice the brief nods of heads, the raised eyebrows, the vague smiles.

He had let them know too, with a sinking heart, that he would probably become surplus to requirements and that his time in their parish would in all likelihood be curtailed. The indifference in the eyes of the bereaved community before him was only to be expected, he'd told himself. He was a temporary fix. A last resort. But it had still hurt.

The expression on Katie's face as she approached him in the sunshine seemed to betray only anguish. He was shocked to find himself hoping that his imminent departure had, at least, upset her. How wrong was that on so many levels, he thought?

Katie had enough on her plate already. The last thing he would want to do was cause her more distress. This poor girl could not live like this indefinitely, he thought.

Constantly looking over her shoulder; fearing the sight of Leonardo's face in a crowd; dreading hearing her name being called out. He had to do something to help her, he resolved. He needed to find out what was going on back in Italy. He had no way of knowing if Father Joseph had attempted enquiries of his own. And he had no idea if his murder had anything to do with Katie's past. But it was a risk he was prepared to take. He had contacts in Puglia. And he was going to make use of them.

'Lovely to see you here today. I'm so sorry for your loss,' he parroted, as he offered his hand to Katie, conscious of the community milling around him. It was only when he saw her crestfallen face that he realised just how formal and impersonal that had sounded. He gripped Katie's fingers awkwardly as their hands met, a strange, empty gesture that failed to express what their eyes disclosed. Acutely aware of the feel of her skin against his, their clasp lingering, Father Luca met her melancholy expression with silence. The right words would just not come, and she removed her hand dejectedly, reluctantly turning away.

'Actually,' he finally found himself calling after Katie before she disappeared amongst the mingling parishioners, the hand of an attractive middle-aged Mediterranean woman already in his, 'I'm going to be snowed under with paperwork for the next couple of weeks until Father Kowalski arrives. I wondered if you'd be available to help out?'

The smile that lit up Katie's face, as she tried not to skip away from the church, hand in hand with Alex, easily outshone her dazzling dress, and even the sun, gloriously resplendent in the sky above.

Maria Fernandez, who had witnessed all of this as she shook Father Luca's hand, had an unreadable expression on her face; utterly inscrutable in fact.

Chapter Twenty-Six

MONDAY

DS Thorne looked uncertain and expectant as DI Sloane stood with his back to him, gazing out of the window of the meeting room. They were alone.

'Thanks for coming in for this meeting today. I think I owe you an explanation,' began Sloane, perching on a desk.

Thorne nodded encouragingly, unsure of the appropriate response.

'If I'm honest, I have had some reservations about you. And I am sure you have your own opinions about me.'

Again, Thorne nodded, this time warily.

'Before I say anything, I have to ask you – why did you access the crime scene alone, without waiting for me? We all know that the victim's mobile phone is missing. Can you understand the position this puts you in?'

'I know. I know. I was an idiot. If I'm honest, I was just trying to impress you, get ahead of the game. I love this job. I've been putting in a lot of hours on this case. My girlfriend is getting a bit fed up actually. So, yeah, I've just been trying to create a good impression. But I think I've probably done the complete opposite to be honest. But I'm not a bent copper, if that's what you're wondering,' Thorne laughed wryly.

'And, for the record, I definitely did not remove a mobile phone from that room. Why would I even do that?'

Sloane sighed. 'Fair enough. I am aware of the effort you are putting in.'

He paused. 'So… It doesn't require an enormous leap of imagination to work out that your search through the files at St Anthony's church uncovered more information than you would have expected. Am I right?'

Thorne caught the Inspector's eye briefly.

'You will have discovered that I attended St Anthony's in the Father O'Leary era? That I was an altar boy there for several years?'

The young sergeant sat in silence; his discomfort was palpable.

'Did your research take you further forward?' asked Sloane.

'To be honest, Sir, there were so many files. You'd need a whole team in there to make any headway.'

'Absolutely. I get that. And don't worry, you won't need to head back there because of me.' Sloane turned to the window again, taking a shaky breath.

'If you had jumped forward just a few short years, you would have found the records for my wedding day. The tenth of May 1990. Sounds corny, but it really was the happiest day of my life. We were really young, but we were so in love. We thought we had our whole lives in front of us. We were going to conquer the world.' Sloane sighed.

'But within three years of becoming my wife, Helen was dead. They threw everything at her when she became unwell; chemo, the lot. Nothing worked. I would spend hours at St Anthony's on my knees, praying, bargaining. I would beg God to take me instead. I had no idea how to deal with all that pain. I was a young copper, fairly new to the job. Didn't know anyone that well. My colleagues had no idea what was going on, and that was how I wanted it.

In case you were wondering, I never met Father Joseph. He arrived a few years after I left. It was Father O'Leary who conducted our wedding service at St Anthony's. And it was Father O'Leary who led my wife's funeral three years later. He was one of the few people who knew what I was going through. Who tried to comfort me. But I turned my back on him and his God. A God who took my wife from me. What had I ever done to deserve that? I'm ashamed to say I can barely bring myself to look at him now. Just hearing his voice seems to bring it all back.

My request for a transfer was granted. With Helen dead and buried, I needed to be as far away as possible from the painful memories, the reminders of the countless trips to our local hospital, Helen sleeping in our small living-room, too weak to use the stairs. I had never been to the West Midlands in my life. I'd never even heard of the town they originally sent me to. I didn't know a soul there. It was perfect.'

'Can I ask why you have come back now, Sir?' Thorne asked gently, still processing facts wildly different from his recent suspicions.

'I suppose a lot of time has passed now. I'm getting older, I'm thinking about retiring soon in all honesty. I've got a couple of sisters with families still in this area. I want to spend a bit of time with them. I was happy enough up there, and the people were lovely. Much friendlier than they are down here really. I never married again though. I tried, but I never really met anybody else that I wanted to settle with. Helen was without doubt the love of my life. And when I eventually go, I want to be buried with her.'

Sloane turned to the window. 'But God, it's been so much harder than I thought it would. Having to deal with a murder at St Anthony's church of all places as soon as I get

94

here. Father O'Leary turning up. It's been torture to be honest.'

A brisk knock on the door rescued Thorne from having to offer a suitably worded response. The sympathy was there; he just lacked the experience in knowing how to convey it.

'Sorry to interrupt,' came a voice from the door, now half open. 'We've just had a call. Nigel Ward is heading back in. He wants to make another statement.'

Chapter Twenty-Seven

An hour later, the three men had resumed the positions in the interview room that they had taken just three days previously. DI Sloane and DS Thorne sat in silence, now uncannily aligned in their stance; upright, alert, expectant. Nigel Ward appeared uncomfortable, fidgeting, adjusting his seat, unable to attain a state of composure, eyes cast nervously downwards.

All at once he raised his head, contemplating the two detectives with despondent eyes.

'I killed someone,' he said, raising his palms as a clear symbol of submission.

'I've killed someone. And I've come to confess.'

Sloane and Thorne exchanged brief glances, a fleeting look enough to convey the fascination they both felt.

Sloane spoke. 'For the record, can you clarify that you are admitting to the murder of Father Joseph Boletti?'

Nigel Ward's features jolted into an expression of shock.

'No! Absolutely not,' he bellowed adamantly. 'No. I did visit him twice to make this confession. But I didn't kill him. I killed someone else.'

Sloane removed the reading glasses that had been perched half way down his nose.

'Mr Ward, can you confirm the name of the person that you did kill then?'

'William Edwards. His name was William Edwards.'

The two detectives looked at him blankly.

'And when exactly did this murder take place?'

'Twenty-two years ago. And it wasn't a murder. I didn't mean to kill the man. I didn't even know him.'

'Mr Ward, before you say any more, we strongly recommend that you find yourself a lawyer. The maximum sentence a judge can impose for manslaughter is life imprisonment. It's a pretty serious charge.'

'I know. I know. And I will. But bearing the weight of this all these years has already made it a life sentence. I have lived with the guilt of what happened that night every single day of my life since then.'

'Twenty-two years is a long time, Mr Ward,' remarked Sloane. 'What has prompted you to come forward after all these years?'

'I've wanted to, for a long time, But, but...' Ward hesitated. 'Well, I didn't. Then, a few months ago, one of my children got sick. Really sick. It was touch and go for a while. Horrendous. I thought we were going to lose him.'

With the back of his hand, Ward wiped at the tears threatening to spill from his eyes. 'It was so out of the blue, so unexpected. He's always been such a healthy young thing. Loves his sport. Football, cricket, swimming. He never even used to get colds. All I could think was that this was my punishment. Sins of the Fathers and all that. I can tell you, my Catholic guilt kicked in big time.'

Sloane peered down at his notes. 'Mr Ward, can you explain to us what exactly happened all those years ago, and how it led to the death of William Edwards?'

Brown closed his eyes momentarily, trying to unsee the horror of that fateful night. 'I was a bit of a tearaway back then. I'd been in the odd bit of trouble with the law. I'd had a few cautions for minor scuffles, being drunk and disorderly, that sort of thing.'

'Yes, we are aware of that. How did things escalate?'

'That night, I'd been to a party miles away, way past Esher, and I stupidly decided to drive back, despite knocking back the drinks all evening. The roads are pretty unlit along some stretches around there, and, of course, I was speeding. I literally didn't see the bicycle until it was too late. I saw a figure go flying, but my foot didn't even touch the brake. It was pure self-preservation. I had my whole life ahead of me. I wanted it all. University, a career, money, a family.

I told myself that people come off bikes all the time. This guy would be fine. What the hell was he doing cycling at night without lights anyway? He was asking for it really. I turned to look behind me, hoping I'd catch a glimpse of a raised fist being shaken at me, a few choice swear words ringing out in the night. But all I could see was an unmoving sheet of darkness.

I got confirmation of the death in local newspaper articles in the following days. A local man in his sixties, who'd had a few himself, but clearly the victim of a hit and run. For weeks, I waited for that knock on the door, bracing myself every time the phone rang. But the call never came. And my life went on as planned.

I somehow managed to put the whole incident to the back of my mind, telling myself the guy only had himself to blame for what had happened.'

Ward lowered his head, defeated.

Sloane nodded slowly, 'So this is what you decided to confess to Father Joseph?'

'Yes.'

'Twice?'

'Yes'

'Why the need to return? Did you miss something out the first time?'

'The first time I went, I really thought that it would be a pretty straightforward process. From what I remembered, you confessed all your sins to the priest, he absolved you, sending you off with some sort of penance, like saying a Hail Mary or two. And that was it. Your slate was clean. You were forgiven. No more guilt to carry around. I knew as sins go, this was a bit of a whopper. But I'd done a bit of research, and I knew that there is this 'sacred seal of confession' and that there was no way the priest was allowed to report me, even if it was a criminal offence.

What I hadn't realised, or expected, was that the priest is allowed to withhold absolution. And that's exactly what Father Joseph did. And more than that – he really wanted me to report my crime to the police. He told me to go away and have a long, hard think about things, and that he would too.

Which is why I went back the following week. It was worth a shot. I just wanted to get rid of the feeling of guilt. I had absolutely no intention of going to the police, of course. To be honest, I was already thinking of alternatives. Charity donations, that sort of thing.

But when I went back the second time, and Father Joseph realised I wasn't prepared to face the legal consequences of what I'd done all those years ago, he started talking about his own moral dilemma and how he had decided to risk excommunication by reporting this.'

'And you are still denying any involvement in the murder of the person who was about to expose your crime to the police?' Sloane's tone betrayed his scepticism.

'Absolutely. That's why I am here now. To set the record straight. I could see how it looked.'

'Can I ask why you chose to come all the way back to St Anthony's church to make this confession?'

'Well, I couldn't really go to my local church, could I? We've had the kids christened there. They go to the local

Catholic primary school. I couldn't risk my voice being recognised.'

Sloane turned to Thorne, conscious that his sergeant would be finding this whole conversation a bit odd. Thorne, however, was not sitting there with a cynical grin on his face. Instead, he was leaning forward over the files on his desk, staring intently at the page open in front of him.

Indeed, he caught both men unawares as he jumped up unexpectedly, excusing himself. Assurances of a swift return were just heard as he disappeared up the corridor towards the meeting room.

'Let's take a short break, shall we? Give you time to collect your thoughts,' suggested Sloane, taking in this unassuming young accountant. This family man. Who knew what dark secrets some people carried?

The question was, how could this all be connected to the murder of Father Joseph? Why would a man confess to being responsible for one death, but deny another? Why did there always have to be a curve ball? Why couldn't a murder case be straightforward, just for once?

DI Sloane was tired. He'd given his life to police work. All that energy in his early career; all that enthusiasm. Where was it now? He almost jumped as the door burst open, and Thorne appeared, his face a picture of triumph. He was still clutching the page that he had removed from the folder to take with him.

'Something interesting, Sir,' he said brightly, as he took his seat opposite Nigel Ward.

'Go ahead,' replied Sloane, feeling something akin to pride.

'Well, I've been browsing through all the information that was pulled up after your interview last week, Mr Ward. I was looking at this newspaper clipping of a local cricket team you played for back in the day, and one of the players' names really rang a bell. Philip Gillingham. I just knew I had seen that name somewhere else. It was really bugging me. And then when you started talking again about coming to confession at St Anthony's, something clicked. That's when I had to go and check the board in the meeting room. Gillingham is the surname of one of our three flower ladies. Quite a coincidence, wouldn't you say?'

A cloud of disquiet shadowed the face of Ward as he cast his eyes down towards the photograph that Thorne had lain in front of him. Eleven beaming, young men in their cricket whites; two rows of them, either standing, hands clasped behind their backs, or seated with their arms folded.

'It was probably cricket that saved me in the end,' Ward admitted, lifting up the photograph to look at it more closely, nostalgia briefly replacing the unease in his eyes. 'They were a great bunch of guys, each and every one of them. They taught me what it meant to be loyal, self-disciplined, a team-player. I learnt so much from them.'

He returned the photograph to Thorne, addressing him directly, 'So, yes, I did know Philip Gillingham. And I do not have a bad word to say about him. I had no idea that he or his family had any connection to St Anthony's church. I wasn't aware that Philip was even a Catholic. In fact, I'm sure he wasn't. Haddelton isn't that big a town. I guess coincidences do happen.'

Sloane raised his eyebrows. 'Mr Ward, can you confirm when you last had any contact with Philip Gillingham? And have you ever met his wife, Maggie?'

Ward met Sloane's expression of incredulity with defiant eyes. 'As you are aware, I left this area over twenty years ago. Never came back after university. I moved on. I needed to. So, let's just say it's been a couple of decades since I had a beer with Philip. And, as far as I am aware, he hadn't even met his future wife when we were playing cricket together.'

'So,' intervened Thorne, 'if we trawl through all the CCTV footage for the roads, say, between St Anthony's church and Mr Gillingham's address on the two Saturdays that you came to Haddelton, are you confident that we are not going to find evidence to the contrary?'

Sloane smiled inwardly.

Nigel Ward, however, clasped his hands behind his head, exhaling with deep frustration. 'Look, okay, I did go and look Philip up the second time I came to Haddelton. I guess curiosity got the better of me. But this guy had absolutely nothing to do with the death of that cyclist. He's a good man. I really didn't want to bring him into this.'

Sloane looked up from what he was jotting down.

'Mr Ward, I don't think I need to remind you that our priority right now is to discover who murdered Father Joseph. And like it or not, you have now created a link to Mr Gillingham.

As far as this hit and run incident from twenty-two years ago is concerned, we literally only have your account of events at the moment. Obviously, we will need to make some further enquiries, and will certainly not be charging you today. You are free to go, but please remain where we can contact you easily. We'll be in touch.'

Chapter Twenty-Eight

TUESDAY

Father Luca smiled as he recognised the lively cocker spaniel he had first encountered outside the church with Katie. He had already become familiar with the route between Father O'Leary's parish church and St Anthony's; the wide, tree-lined roads, the elegant Victorian architecture, the spacious 1930s properties. An Englishman's home was certainly his castle around here, he thought.

It took a good half hour to walk it, but he had little else to do. Weekday masses were suspended while enquiries were ongoing. And for some reason, Father Joseph had no weddings or christenings booked in until August. What had the poor man known? Had he predicted his own death? Had he been dicing with danger somehow?

Trying to keep his mind occupied, Father Luca was filling his time reorganising the parish office. He was keeping his fingers crossed that no one in the parish suddenly and unexpectedly needed a funeral. He'd never done one of those. Father Joseph's, of course, would be on hold for now and out of his hands anyway.

As he neared the excited dog, now pulling on its lead, eager and curious, Father Luca's thoughts turned to Katie, remembering his friend's smile as she'd patted its head. Was she his friend now? She was in his head all the time. But surely that was because he wanted to help her. She was a parishioner in distress. It all came under the umbrella of ministerial duties, didn't it? And she could be a useful ally for him too. Give him a bit of support.

Yet, for some reason, he felt exposed, wary, vulnerable even. A fissure had appeared in his granite-like vocation.

He was yet to contact Katie.

'What's your dog called?' he asked laughing, as the affectionate animal jumped up, pinning him to the large hedge behind him.

'Buddy,' replied its owner, smiling, pulling on the lead apologetically. 'Buddy by name, buddy by nature,' he grinned. It was not the first time he had made his quip.

Buddy, like Father Luca, heard the gentle thud in the earth beneath the hedge that was threatening to engulf the young priest, and turned his attentions, in the fickle manner of dogs, to his next discovery. But it was Father Luca who spotted the concealed object first, inanimate, intact, camouflaged by the dark, entwined branches of the hedge and the shaded earth below it.

Father Luca turned to his companion. 'You don't have any tissues or a spare bag, do you?' he asked.

'Is the Pope a Catholic?' the man replied laughing, extracting a poo bag and some thick tissue from his pocket. His expression altered dramatically as he handed them over. 'Oh, sorry Father. No offence intended.'

'None taken,' replied Father Luca smiling, before he bent down and very carefully retrieved the dislodged mobile phone that had revealed itself beside a pavement a short walk away from St Anthony's church.

Once back in Father Joseph's study, having delicately carried his find along the streets of Haddelton, the offerings of his invisible dog, Father Luca opened up the large diary on the now considerably tidier desk. Every fibre of his being told him that he should be heading directly for the police station.

As far as he knew, Father Joseph's mobile phone was still missing. He'd put two and two together when he'd realised the police had no contact details whatsoever for him. The likelihood that this phone contained vital information was overwhelming. Yet he was sure that without a PIN number, the police would struggle to access all this information. Wouldn't they? He continued to flick through the thick pages of the diary until he reached the entry that had confused him.

On the fourteenth of July, in small, faint letters, the words *pin it up* had been written in. When combing through Father Joseph's plans for the weeks following his murder, Father Luca had not quite understood what exactly needed to be displayed on that day. But now, with this newly found mobile phone in his possession, he wondered whether Father Joseph had actually been capable of some vaguely shrewd encryption. With some thin tissue covering the tip of his finger, Father Luca pressed the narrow button at the side of the phone to turn it on. The battery, he noted gratefully, still had charge on it. He then double-checked the date of that particular entry, the fourteenth of July, and carefully typed in the numbers 1-4-0-7 as the PIN.

As the phone unlocked, its screen displaying the usual array of icons, Father Luca froze. Now, surely, was the time to hand in this evidence to the police? Was he perverting the course of justice now? But his curiosity got the better of him. Just one more step, he told himself, as he pressed the small square at the bottom of the screen, bringing up any recent unclosed pages. Just to be sure. And that would be it.

As he slowly digested the words that revealed themselves, bewildering, startling, extraordinary, Father

Luca sat down, dumbfounded. Eventually, he slowly placed the tissue-clad phone back on the desk, and gazed towards the window for a few moments, deep in thought. Abruptly, he began to scramble through the various papers and folders that he had been so recently reorganising.

Father Luca was looking for an address. He had a visit to make.

Chapter Twenty-Nine

DI Sloane looked across at DS Thorne sitting on the other side of the station office, head bent forward at a computer, his searching eyes glued to the screen, fingers tapping lightly, pausing only to scribble occasionally in his notebook, never far from his side. Contrary to his initial expectations, Sloane had to admit that his sergeant had definitely proved himself in the last few days. If he had been trying to impress him, he was certainly doing a great job of it.

Possibly sensing the Inspector's eyes on him, Thorne glanced up and called across to Sloane, 'Sir, I've found something you might want to see.'

Sloane smiled as he joined him. 'What have you got for me now, Sherlock?'

'Well, firstly, the hit and run details all check out. No one was ever charged with the man's death. The only possible clue to the vehicle responsible was a small flake of red paint found on the frame of the mangled bicycle. We would really only have Nigel Ward's word as evidence that he was involved. I'm not sure it would be enough to bring it to the CPS. Especially as it turns out that he didn't actually pass his driving test until the following year. And wasn't the registered or named driver of a vehicle until then.'

Sloane nodded. 'Well done. I think our Mr Ward is going to have to do an awful lot of charity work to find some peace of mind by the looks of it.'

'Except.' Thorne pulled up another page onto the screen. 'What is very interesting, according to records here, is that

Philip Gillingham had passed his driving test by then, and that he had bought himself a little car. A little, red car, funnily enough. He got stopped for speeding once. Surprise, surprise. There's a bit of paperwork on it on file.'

'Brilliant work. We need to get hold of Mr Gillingham now. Bring forward any meeting already arranged with him. We need to speak to him today. I think Nigel Ward has been supplying us with half-truths, trying not to implicate anyone else. I have a feeling that he wasn't the only person in the car that night. And if Philip Gillingham has got wind of this, who knows what he could have done to protect himself?'

Chapter Thirty

'Father Luca. What a surprise. What can I do for you? Would you like to come in?'

Maria Fernandez's face betrayed a wariness as she motioned for Father Luca to enter her narrow hallway, closing the door quietly and carefully behind him.

'Do sit down,' she offered, indicating the armchair in the corner of her living room. The room was dim with the curtains almost fully drawn, a narrow chink of sunlight providing what little brightness existed in there, illuminating the specks of dust that danced aimlessly within it.

'Miss Fernandez,' began Father Luca, looking helplessly towards the door, feelings of regret and doubt setting in. What was he thinking? What did he hope to achieve that the police couldn't?

Yet, as his eyes met the expression of utter anguish and heartache on the face of the woman sat opposite him, he understood in that moment that sometimes the heart instinctively knows best.

'Miss Fernandez, I have come into possession of some information. I will have to pass it all onto the police in due course. But I felt that you needed to be made aware of something.'

From the darkness of her sofa, Maria watched, intrigued, as Father Luca pulled out the mobile phone from a small bag that he had with him. Recognition dawned on her face as he unfolded the tissue to reveal the screen. 'You've got Father Joseph's phone?' she asked tearfully.

'Yes,' replied Father Luca hesitantly. 'And there is something you need to see before I hand it over.'

'I don't understand. Father Joseph and I never communicated by mobile phone. It was always in person. I'm not sure what you could have found on there that has anything to do with me.'

'Would you like to have a look?' suggested Father Luca, offering the phone to Maria.

'Oh, I'm far too vain to put on my reading glasses in front of a handsome young Italian man,' she laughed. 'But I am happy for you to read out whatever it is.'

'Only if you're sure. It's basically a draft of a text message not yet sent. It looks like it was the last thing Father Joseph had used his phone for before... Before it was taken.'

Luca positioned the phone in front of him, its screen lighting up his face in the gloom.

'Would the fourteenth of July be of any particular significance to Father Joseph, do you know?' he asked, tapping in the PIN.

'It's my birthday actually,' replied Maria, a note of curiosity entering her voice.

Father Luca nodded, understanding, and began to read.

'My dear Maria. My love. Forgive me. Forgive me for all these years. Forgive me for my indecision, my selfishness, my inability to put you first. I have tried to serve God, but I was not prepared to lose you. By wanting you both, I have failed you, and I have failed God. But I have loved you from the moment I set eyes on you, all those years ago, and I will never be able to stop loving you, Maria.

I have made a decision to do something which will mean my position in the Church is no longer tenable. I do not wish for you to be caught up in any details in this matter. That's why I'm putting this message in writing, to avoid your questions and keep you safe.

But I want you to know one thing, Maria. The reason I am leaving the Church is to be with you. Forgive me for making you wait all these years. For so long, I have needed to make a choice. But now finally, amore mio, I choose you.'

They sat in silence for a few moments, Luca all too aware of the cruel timing of this revelation.

'I'm so sorry about all of this,' he finally ventured.

'Thank you,' replied Maria, dabbing her eyes. 'He was a good man, a very good man. Please do not think badly of him. He did his best. That's all any of us can do, isn't it? He was so full of love. Joseph's love was of such magnitude that it spilled over, enveloping me in its sweet warmth. What we had was a celebration of tenderness and devotion. Please don't see it as a weakness or a failure.'

With that, she stood up and pulled back the curtains, allowing the sunlight to flood in. Her eyes glistened with emotion as she watched Father Luca place the phone carefully back into his bag.

'I'm going to have to take this to the police now. I hope you understand. Actually, did you want me to take a photograph of the message with my phone before I go?'

Maria shook her head. 'No, I don't want you getting yourself into trouble on my account. Let's both forget that you paid me this little visit, shall we? I will remember Joseph's message for the rest of my life. To be honest, my heart is both weeping and singing right now. I have lost Joseph. But I won his heart in the end.'

She hesitated. 'Between you and me, I did manage to obtain a little something to treasure. Joseph was always so strict about keeping everything secret. The police will have found no trace of me at the presbytery, no clue as to my presence in his life.'

Maria's face darkened. 'Walking into that room and finding Joseph's lifeless body was the most awful moment of my life. I called his name over and over, scrambling for my phone in my bag. It was when I was speaking to the emergency services, trying to make sense of what had happened, that I spotted the two photographs. Shots from a recent parish trip to Walsingham. One was a group shot, all of us, arm in arm, laughter all round. The other was of Joseph, relaxed in the sunshine, his kind eyes smiling, so handsome, so brimming with life.

I knew there was a chance that I would never see that photograph again. That it would be bagged up and stored away in a dark cupboard somewhere, its value reduced to nothing more than a piece of evidence.

So I grabbed at the photos, to have something of Joseph. I did it without thinking. In my panic, I sprayed and wiped the table, worried that my fresh fingerprints would implicate me. Rather silly of me, I know. But I wasn't thinking straight.'

'Well, I guess we're partners in crime now, aren't we?' replied Father Luca. 'Your secret is safe with me.'

As he rose to leave, Maria approached him, cupping his face in her hands. 'Father, I thank you from the bottom of my heart for what you have done today. You are a good man. But please bear something in mind. It is sadly too late for me. It isn't for you.'

Maybe Father Luca was lost in deep thought as he left Maria's and started to walk in the direction of the police station; perhaps it was the fact that Elizabeth was wearing large, dark glasses. After all, he'd only met her the once. Whatever the reason, he failed to recognise the woman with the blonde ponytail and immaculate trainers as Katie's friend. And she was heading purposefully in the direction of Katie's flat.

Chapter Thirty-One

DI Sloane's car drew to a halt outside the Gillinghams' home, overlooking the vast playing fields of a local primary school. It always mystified him why people needed to live in houses as palatial as this, with their high ceilings and enormous sash windows. The maintenance, the cleaning, the heating bills. Was it all worth it? How much space did people really need? He knew this couple only had two children, so there were probably more bathrooms than occupants of this property. Did they even use all the living rooms? Or did the house just enable a dysfunctional existence, estranged individuals masquerading as a contented family unit? He smiled. Maybe he was just jealous.

He turned to Thorne, 'Right, let's hear what our Mr Gillingham has got to say about all of this.'

The crunch of their footsteps on the gravel driveway announced the arrival of the two detectives before they even reached the wide, glossy front door. Philip Gillingham, smiling welcomingly, greeted them with a firm handshake each.

'Come in, officers, we'll go through to my study,' he said, indicating a doorway off the large, elegantly furnished hallway, all herringbone flooring and tastefully framed art.

'It's fortunate I was working from home today. I travel quite a bit with my job, so I'm not always around,' Gillingham explained, as he sat down confidently behind his heavy wooden desk, gesturing for the two men to take the seats in front of it.

'So, how can I be of assistance today?' he continued, looking at the detectives expectantly. 'I am obviously aware of last week's tragedy up at the church. I have to say I'm a strictly christenings, weddings and funerals man, so didn't really know the poor chap that died. I know my wife had been very upset about the whole matter though. Nasty business.'

'Mr Gillingham,' Sloane ventured. 'Can I just confirm your whereabouts last Wednesday morning?'

Philip Gillingham looked at the Inspector with astonishment. And then outrage.

'I beg your pardon?'

'It is standard police procedure to eliminate as many people as possible from our enquiry. You are not being singled out here. We are just routinely establishing all the facts.'

'Well, I am very pleased to hear that. Nevertheless, I am really at pains to understand why you even feel the need to eliminate me from your enquiry. What possible motive would I have for murdering my wife's parish priest? Jealousy? Too many flower-arranging sessions up at the church?'

Gillingham started to laugh. 'Look I have no reason to suspect that Maggie was having an affair with the man. None whatsoever. Is this why you wanted to speak to me before my wife? She's quite put out you know; quite cross that you contacted me instead of her. Presumably you'll be wanting to eliminate her from your enquiries too? Or does all that church going give her a free pass? She's hovering somewhere in the house if you want to get it over and done with. Probably listening at the door right now, to be honest.'

'We will, of course, be speaking to Mrs Gillingham in due course,' Sloane assured him. 'But for the record, could

115

you please clarify where you were last Wednesday morning?'

Gillingham bristled. 'For the record,' he parroted, 'I was in Zurich all day Wednesday. I flew out Tuesday evening and returned Thursday evening.

And I'm sure the airport authorities will be able to confirm all the details for you,' he added with a triumphant flourish.

As Thorne busied himself noting this all down, Sloane knew that it was time to play his ace card.

'There was another reason for wanting to speak to you today, Mr Gillingham. We understand that a Mr Nigel Ward came to see you recently. Can you confirm this to be true, and if so, can you describe the nature of your meeting please?'

Sloane noticed with satisfaction that Gillingham had clearly been caught out by this line of enquiry.

'Nigel?' Gillingham repeated, struggling to regain his composure. 'What on earth has he got to do with anything?'

'Can you confirm that you have spoken to him recently?'

'I literally had not seen the guy for years. He lives somewhere out the back of beyond, I think. But, yes, he turned up on my doorstep a couple of weeks back. Out of the blue. Didn't recognise him at first.'

'Can I ask what you spoke about?' asked Sloane.

'This and that. Said he happened to be in the area and thought he'd look me up. We reminisced about our cricketing days. We used to play cricket together. That's how I know him. Maggie made us a quick cup of tea. He didn't stay that long really. I was very busy with work, as always.'

'Did Mr Ward mention anything in connection with St Anthony's church?'

'He didn't. But goodness. Is he a suspect? Is that why you are here? Did he use me as a cover, do you think? A reason to be in Haddelton?'

Gillingham was doing a grand job of appearing to be speculating earnestly, thought Sloane.

'Mr Gillingham,' continued Sloane, now shifting in his seat. 'I understand that you had not been in touch for a good while, but I know that you and Mr Ward go back a long way. I'd like you to cast your mind back quite some time for me. Can you confirm that you purchased your first car in 1999, a red car, and that you were the registered owner for the following three years?'

At this, Gillingham froze and closed his eyes in despair. He was an overly confident man, who lacked self-awareness at times. But he wasn't stupid.

'My God. He's told you, hasn't he?'

Sloane nodded silently.

'I couldn't believe it when he turned up like that, in a complete state, scared stiff because this priest was threatening to spill the beans. What an idiot, telling someone after all this time. I'd told him to go back again, make every promise under the sun. Delay things for a while. I was hoping the priest was calling his bluff to be honest.

Then when I heard about the murder, I really thought that Nigel had done it. He'd been desperate. Didn't know which way to turn. And I can see why you've come knocking at my door. But I am telling you now. I had nothing to do with that priest's murder. In fact, I've been half wondering if I'm next on the list?'

Sloane sighed. 'Nigel Ward has a solid alibi for last Wednesday too, so we are currently reserving judgement on his involvement in Father Joseph's death. Although we are ruling nothing out at this stage, of course.

117

However, we do need you to accompany us to the station now to make a statement about events from twenty-two years ago. I suggest you get yourself a good lawyer.'

Defeated, Philip Gillingham led the two detectives out into the hall.

'I need to let Maggie know what's going on,' he explained, gesturing with his head in the direction of the kitchen.

Maggie was waiting rigidly, not far inside the kitchen doorway, her face riddled with bewilderment and fear. She looked from one man to the other, observing their expressions of pity and concern.

'I've got to go down to the station, Mags. Things are pretty serious I'm afraid.' Gillingham's tone of voice revealed his despair.

'No!' she cried. 'No, this can't be happening. You were in Zurich last week. What the hell is going on here?'

'It's something else. I didn't want to worry you with it.'

'Worry me? I've thought of nothing else since that dreadful man came round. I didn't catch all of it, but I heard enough to know he'd found himself with his back against the wall, with Father Joseph holding the gun to his head. I could see where this was heading and you would have ended up in the firing line too. I just don't understand. I thought it was all going to be okay now.' Maggie began to weep.

'What do you mean, Mags?' asked Gillingham, clearly confused, moving into the kitchen to reach for a tissue.

With perfect synchronicity, both detectives glanced across the cavernous room for the first time, catching sight of the large vase of sunflowers, drooping now, past their best, reflected so splendidly in the gleaming, black granite surface of Maggie Gillingham's kitchen island.

Chapter Thirty-Two

It had all been so easy really. Considering I was a beginner. And I couldn't do any research online obviously. That would have been a bit of a giveaway.

But I did really think it through. I was pretty meticulous in my planning, particularly when it came to covering my tracks. For a start, it was timed to perfection, putting any number of people in the frame, while hopefully ruling out the obvious candidates. Philip wasn't even in the country that day. Apart from anything else, I'd wanted to be sure he had a rock-solid alibi.

I knew that numbers at weekday masses were low, but surely high enough to give the police something to get their teeth into for a while. And I realised that most of the people in attendance were frail, elderly and devout. But, after all those years on this planet, and all that interaction with St Anthony's church, surely there were a few skeletons in the closet to work on.

I'd both revelled in and cringed at my masterly attempts to disguise myself. The weather was thankfully on my side; dull, cool, drizzly. I had discreetly scoured the charity shops with great success. Who knew there were so many of them around? The hooded polyester anorak I had chosen was something I wouldn't normally be seen dead in. Unfortunate turn of phrase there, I suppose.

I'd had great fun deciding which cardboard mask I would use. A whole raft of celebrities and Royals had been in the running. But it was Henry VIII that I finally chose. Again, I thought it might help throw the police off the scent if the old man ended up surviving. They'd all be attributing it to religious-based terrorism with any luck.

Of course, I'd brought some plastic gloves with me. There would be no tell-tale fingerprints on that hefty paper knife I'd seen displayed, unused, just sitting there really. I wasn't going to make that glaringly obvious mistake of buying a large knife shortly before the crime. Again, presumably a bit of a giveaway once the police start getting into details. And I certainly wasn't going to bring one from home, leaving me either with that telling gap in my array of gleaming kitchen blades, or stubborn blood stains, detectable under that blue light they always use in police dramas as they finally outwit the suspect.

I'd dawdled near the church, unseen, watching the churchgoers leave, waiting until I was sure it was empty. I knew Maria Fernandez would probably be returning at some point, so I didn't have long. She was always very territorial about her Wednesdays. But she'd told me on Sunday that her sick cat would be keeping her otherwise occupied this week. To be honest, I couldn't believe my luck. I just knew it was now or never.

I'd brought along some fresh sunflowers as a cover, just in case I was accosted by a lingering parishioner, kneeling before a lit candle or something. I'd just play the innocent flower lady with rehearsed, altruistic claims of wanting to brighten up the church in this gloomy weather.

Slipping in and ascertaining that I was indeed alone, I'd kept my hood raised, pulled on my gloves and positioned the cardboard mask over my face, flinging the redundant sunflowers onto a front pew. I knew Father Joseph would be in the sacristy at this point, and I wasted no time reaching that heavy, wooden door. I couldn't allow any doubts to enter my head. The man deserved everything that was coming to him. He bent the rules to suit himself. A hypocrite, willing to destroy the lives of others, to jeopardise my children's future, to tear apart my family life. I had to do this. I had to extinguish the sparks that threatened to burn down my life, my children's lives. My children's education. Yes, I supposed this was premeditated murder. But don't they say the end justifies the means? Or had I got that wrong?

Creeping in, I'd taken Father Joseph by surprise that morning as he stood there, head bent over his phone, tapping slowly with one finger. He had barely seen me before I plunged in the blade, grabbed swiftly from its usual position. Interestingly, he'd managed to place his phone in a prominent position on a pile of hymn books before curling forward, clutching his stomach, finally falling backwards with a sickening thud.

I heard the fall rather than saw it, as I implemented my master stroke, hurriedly spraying a large eye on the wall with some paint I had quietly acquired from the PFA cupboard at school. No one would notice it missing for a couple of days. But goodness, a symbol left behind on the wall would surely send the police into a frenzy. I couldn't believe I'd thought of it. I was such a genius. It was going to waste hours of their time.

The importance that Father Joseph had seemed to give to his phone had worried me; the intensity with which he had been concentrating on it; the way he had managed to get it onto that table. I knew that I hadn't any unusual, remotely incriminating phone contact with him. And neither had Philip. But what if somebody else had? Or what if he had left some sort of last-minute clue?

I'd had no time to think clearly at that point, so I'd scooped up the phone, switching it off and popping it in the pocket of the anorak. The dreadful jacket, of course, would shortly be finding itself hanging on the rails of a charity shop, some distance from the one it was purchased from. Any stains on the dark blue polyester, blood or otherwise, would be considered all part and parcel of most of the insalubrious items they received, I would imagine. As for the mask, I would be shredding that as soon as I got home.

I'd remembered to snatch up the sunflowers. I wasn't going to be traced by my visit to the florist's that morning. Unfortunately, leaving with the phone belonging to Father Joseph had clearly not been part of my plan. The item had needed to be disposed of as quickly as possible. Obviously, the further away from the church I got, the better.

However, a passing police car had unnerved me and I'd been forced to thrust the phone deep into the next suitable hedge, overgrown, tangled, sharp, hoping that it would never be seen again. Particularly as I had removed the plastic gloves by then. Did rainfall wash off fingerprints?

So that was it really. Mission accomplished. I'd ride out the inevitable storm. Plant a few seeds of suspicion maybe.

And everything would be okay.

Chapter Thirty-Three

SIX MONTHS LATER

'Ladies and Gentlemen, we have begun our descent into Ancona airport. Please turn off all portable devices…'

Neither Katie nor Alex was really listening to the announcement. Alex, in the window seat, gazed down curiously as the rough, grey sea beneath them was met by a glorious white landscape, which then grew ever closer, until they were part of it, brakes roaring, the plane eventually juddering to a halt.

Katie peered out of the window over Alex's head, remembering the last time she had seen Italy from a plane. She had never wanted to set eyes on the place again. She certainly hadn't imagined herself returning within three years, bringing Alex too. But things were different now.

The aftermath of Father Joseph's death had made for a turbulent summer. Katie had initially found it almost impossible to believe that one of her best friends was capable of murder. The gleeful whispers at the school gate had infuriated her. Not until confirmation had started to trickle through of bail conditions and court dates had Katie been forced to accept the grim reality. It had shaken her to the core. To think that Maggie had plied her with suggestions that Elizabeth was the culprit instead.

Katie had managed to confront Elizabeth directly about Olivia's father the day she had popped in for coffee. Anticipating reluctance, she had been relieved at the snorts of laughter that had met her gentle questioning. And, as it turned out, there was nothing remotely sinister about her teenage pregnancy. A family holiday in Bournemouth; Elizabeth, an innocent, naïve fifteen-year-old; an unexpectedly exciting evening spent in the company of some equally young international students, drinking cider. Her behaviour had been ill-judged, but complicit. She'd barely been able to pronounce the boy's name, let alone recall whereabouts in Spain he was from. Her one mistake was going to cost her dearly. But she didn't feel the need to ruin someone else's life, even if she were in a position to.

Katie and Elizabeth had tried to support each other as the repercussions of the murder had unfolded around them. Fortunately for all concerned, Elizabeth had never come to know that she'd been a pawn in Maggie's game. Katie had wisely decided not to share that little blip in the history of their friendship. Or the fact that she'd kept herself as near as possible to the door of her flat, mobile phone in hand, the day that Elizabeth had come over for coffee. Just in case.

Instead, they'd sat together in disbelief over endless coffees, dissecting all the conversations they'd ever had with Maggie. Looking for clues, hints that she would have gone to such lengths. If they were honest, there hadn't been any. They'd always talked about how they'd do anything for their children. But committing murder? It was unbelievable. They were both as shocked as each other.

The situation with Father Luca had not been quite as straightforward. Katie had only really seen him a few times before he left, and he'd usually been a bit distracted, distant even.

And yet. He had eventually contacted Katie about helping him with the sort-out of Father Joseph's study. Even if he seemed to have done a pretty good job of it already. She'd caught him watching her once when she'd looked up suddenly from something she'd been reading, trying to decide where on earth it should be filed. He'd hurriedly asked her if she felt okay as she looked a little pale. Which was strange, as her suntan was coming along nicely by then. He'd also been amazingly good at remembering her favourite biscuits and how she liked her tea. Even if he had then suddenly had to busy himself with a task elsewhere, taking his own tea with him. He'd never appeared to take the slightest bit of notice of the clothes she'd put on or how she'd worn her hair. Yet he'd taken himself off to a barber's once to tame his own mop of hair. It must have been just before she'd come over. She could tell by the little snippets of hair, fair against his black shirt, scattered over his shoulders. And the fact that his hair had looked great.

She, of course, hadn't been remotely aware that Father Luca was still busy making enquiries about Leonardo. After Maggie's arrest, he'd got a bit bolder, eventually uncovering the fatal overdose and subsequent funeral of a man consumed with self-hatred at the weakness that had cost him his wife and son, but ultimately unable to conquer it. Leonardo had been dead for nearly a year.

Katie recalled the day that Father Luca had broken the news to her. So gently, so tenderly. Instinctively knowing that a hug would serve far better than meaningless platitudes. She had found it impossible to understand why a person so tactile and loving would choose such a solitary path, such a lonely existence.

The young priest's departure a short time later had left a huge hole in her life. She knew that he had to follow the path he'd chosen. She guessed that it just wasn't meant to be. But without him around, she had felt so lost.

125

Katie had also found that she was starting to miss Italy. As tragic as Leonardo's death had been, it had effectively set her free. She had begun to fill Alex in on his forgotten early childhood, his loving grandparents, the wonderful years that she and daddy had spent in Rome. No more secrets. No more lies. It was utterly liberating.

When Father Luca's name had lit up on her buzzing phone that afternoon in late September, Katie had answered the call with curiosity, trying to ignore the surge of delight that had run through her. To hear his voice again after all this time had been wonderful. Yet his words had been disappointingly fleeting, a little muddled. She would receive a text message from him on her phone, and he hoped she understood.

Katie had read Father Luca's words so often that she knew them off by heart. She had been caught entirely unawares, having accepted his lengthy silence as an indication of his determination to follow his calling, and to leave behind the unwanted distractions of the summer.

So, the news of his decision to leave the seminary had come as a considerable shock to her. His explanation was brief. He'd come to realise that he was running away from something rather than moving towards something. In fact, it was Katie he was running from. And he didn't want to run from her any longer.

And now a Christmas holiday in Italy lay ahead. Spent with Luca and his family. Even after all the phone calls and messages, Katie couldn't quite believe that she was going to see Father Luca again. Although that wasn't strictly true, of course, was it? Would it be strange addressing him as Luca? What would he even look like in jeans and a t-shirt? Katie smiled. Just fine, she imagined. As long as he still wore those lovely suede desert boots.

She had the distinct feeling that Luca's parents would be welcoming her and Alex with open arms. By all accounts, they'd stocked up on enough *panettone, panforte* and *prosecco* to last until next Christmas. Though, if the truth be told, Alex was perhaps more excited about meeting their dog than anything else.

Significantly, the trip would also involve a visit from Alex's grandparents, overjoyed at the prospect of being reunited with their grandson. It had taken a while, but Katie had finally plucked up the courage to call Leonardo's parents, her hands trembling, her heart racing. Her shaky explanations had been met solely with apologies and grateful tears. Because of Alex, they were family, and, knowing that they would be a source of comfort to each other, they were all keen to keep the many happy memories alive, for Alex's sake as much as theirs.

Katie leant over and hugged Alex. 'You know *Nonno* and *Nonna* don't speak any English. Can you remember how to say Happy Christmas in Italian?'

'Of course I can. *Buon Natale!*' laughed Alex.

'*Buon Natale*, Alessio.'

Chapter Thirty-Four

'I can't believe how early it gets dark at the moment. Catches me out every year. It's literally only four o'clock,' DS Thorne laughed, holding the pub door open for DI Sloane as they headed inside towards the warmth, tinsel, and Noddy Holder on a loop. Early Christmas Eve revellers were already bunched around tables in their novelty snowman ear-rings, and jumpers with sparkling seasonal messages.

'The nights will be drawing out before you know it,' replied Sloane, nodding towards a small table beside a fireplace covered in fairy lights. 'Grab that and I'll get the drinks in.'

From his position at the bar, squeezed in amongst the patiently waiting customers, full of determined good cheer, Sloane looked across at his colleague, now sat with his head down, checking his phone. Not the thorn in his side he'd expected in the end. Perhaps they were the cliché he'd been so determined not to be. And maybe that wasn't such a bad thing after all.

'I hope that's not work,' Sloane said, as he placed Thorne's pint in front of him, froth gliding down the glass, reaching his thumb.

'No, it's Emily messaging me. Making sure I'm going to be on time this evening. She's cooking me dinner. A romantic evening in on Christmas Eve, who'd have thought? The lion has been tamed,' he laughed.

'You take care of her. Make plenty of time for her. She's been good for you. There's more to life than solving crimes.'

'Yeah, you're right. But we've had a good run this year, haven't we? That case back in the summer was a shocker. I think that poor woman is going to go down for quite some time for killing that priest. Their expensive lawyers may have got the husband's case dismissed. I guess it was his word against Nigel Ward's. And with none of the original evidence left after all this time, it would have been a hard one to prove. But Maggie Gillingham is definitely up against it. What with the sunflowers placing her at the scene of the crime, not to mention her fingerprints all over the phone that the young priest handed in. She hasn't really got a leg to stand on. Her poor kids. They are the ones who are going to suffer just as much as her.'

'Indeed. I don't know what she was thinking. We didn't see that one coming, did we? That poor priest. Just trying to follow his conscience. Loved England. Made it his home. Only changed his name to Father Joseph because none of his parishioners ever seemed to be able to pronounce or spell his Italian name properly. All he wanted was a quiet life, by all accounts. Tried to do his best by everybody, and look what happened. Poor chap.'

Sloane took a sip of his beer. 'Still, against all the odds, we've turned out to be pretty decent partners in crime. Once we got the measure of each other, I guess.' He smiled wryly.

Thorne grinned. 'I know I probably came over as a bit of an idiot at times. But I've learnt loads from you, Sir. I know I've got a whole lot more to learn, so I'm hoping you're not building up to a resignation announcement here.' He glanced warily at his boss.

'You know what, I think I've got a couple more years left in me yet,' laughed Sloane.

'That's brilliant news. Best Christmas present I've had so far. Cheers! Happy Christmas.'

Sloane met Thorne's glass, held up towards him in celebration.

'Happy Christmas, Harry.'

Chapter Thirty-Five

Maria Fernandez leant down to switch on the fairy lights that twinkled brightly on the dainty tree in the corner of her living room. The tree cast a warm glow across the room, illuminating her fireplace, wreathed in fresh holly and mistletoe, Christmas card perfect.

Maria's hands were still cold after walking back the short distance from Christmas Day Mass, the festive hymns still ringing in her ears. Father Kowalski seemed amiable enough, though his sermons were perhaps a little too long and rambling for her liking. And he always seemed determined to raise a laugh. Which was no bad thing, she supposed, but perhaps their sense of humours differed. Fortunately, she only attended Mass on Sundays these days.

A sharp knock on her front door startled her as she carefully poured herself a solitary sherry.

'Doreen?' she exclaimed as she opened the door, icy air streaming into her hallway. 'Is everything okay?'

'Everything is absolutely fine, my dear. The turkey is looking wonderful and the spuds are coming along a treat. I've left my daughter in charge for a bit. Though the grandchildren are already bouncing off the ceiling with the excitement of it all,' laughed Doreen.

'Come on in. I thought I'd have a little sherry here before I headed next door to you. I didn't want to arrive too early in case I got in the way,' explained Maria. But she looked confused as she eyed the parcel in Doreen's hand.

'I just wanted to give you this while we had a bit of peace and quiet,' said Doreen, handing her a beautifully wrapped gift.

Maria was touched. 'Will you join me for a sherry while I open it? This is so kind of you.'

It seemed a shame to tear at the neatly presented offering in its thick, seasonal wrapping paper, all smiling Santas and cheery reindeer. Maria did her best to preserve what she could of the paper, sliding the present out cautiously.

'A photo frame. How beautiful!' Maria cried, looking down admiringly at the antique brass surround, appreciative of her neighbour's kind gesture. It was only when she raised her head and caught Doreen's eye, observing the teary emotion, the unconditional sympathy, and the utter lack of judgement, that she understood the significance of this gift.

'Now, are you going to do it, or shall I?' asked Doreen, smiling, as she turned to Maria's bookshelf with its tidy rows of small, neat paperbacks. On closer inspection, it did seem strange that all the classics and poetry were flanked by a sizeable, well-thumbed, hardback copy of Colleen McCullough's *The Thorn Birds*.

'Talk about hiding things in plain sight,' she laughed kindly.

'And it's lucky I'm a Shirley Bassey fan too,' she added. 'These walls aren't that thick, you know. I think I know every word of "Never, Never, Never". And the Italian version too. Such a beautiful song. It wasn't hard to put two and two together. I've never known anyone to go to church so much.'

Doreen glanced over to where Maria's precious photographs lay hidden. 'I've never pried, rest assured, but I have spotted them on occasions. Unlike those two clowns that came round. It didn't take much guesswork to work out what you were hiding.'

Maria smiled coyly, looking down at the photo frame in her lap. 'The gift is perfect, thank you. It's going to look beautiful on my shelf. I just hope you don't hear me talking to Joseph and think I'm mad. It's really going to help me. Until I'm reunited with him.'

She looked up, her eyes full of emotion. 'You see, Doreen, it's Joseph's turn to wait for me now.'

The two friends raised their sherry glasses and smiled through their tears.

'*Feliz Navidad*, Doreen.'

'*Feliz Navidad*, Maria.'